67596
TO
Grace
Episcopal Church)
with love,
Nancy
Blakey

MORE

MUDPIES:

101

ALTERNATIVES

TO

TELEVISION

by Nancy Blakey

TRICYCLE PRESS
Berkeley, California

To Greg

~

"Imagination is more important than knowledge, for knowledge is limited, whereas imagination embraces the entire world— stimulating progress, giving birth to evolution."

—Albert Einstein

TRICYCLE PRESS
P.O. Box 7123
Berkeley, California 94707

Illustrations by Melissah Watts
Book design by Watts Design

Library of Congress Cataloging-in-Publication Data
Blakey, Nancy.
    More mudpies : 101 alternatives to television / Nancy Blakey.
        p.   cm.
    Includes index.
    ISBN 1-883672-11-2
    1. Handicraft—Juvenile literature. 2. Science—Experiments—
Juvenile literature. [1. Handicraft. 2. Science—Experiments.
3. Experiments.] I. Title.
TT160.B53 1994
649'.51—dc20   94-11709
                                                     CIP
                                                     AC

First Tricycle Press printing, 1994
Manufactured in the United States of America

1 2 3 4 5 6 — 98 97 96 95 94

Contents

How This Book Began

It was nothing more than a tree, the claimed territory of my children, that made me turn off the television. TV had slipped into our family when we began having babies, helping me to survive. Many mornings I drowsed in front of "Sesame Street" nursing the latest, knowing the others were secured to the set. Sometimes I pushed in a short cartoon video after "Sesame Street" for uninterrupted housework. Nothing much, nothing bad. But then the dreaded dinner hour approached, the hour when kids are biologically programmed to be ornery and restless. Preparing a decent meal with tiny arms and legs wrapped fretfully around me seemed impossible. Click! Late afternoon cartoons, a "Sesame Street" repeat, and Mr. Rogers. Simple as that. Nearly four hours of TV a day. I scarcely gave it a thought. The television seemed a household necessity, like a washing machine or a clock radio.

The summer after our fourth child was born, we decided to take a vacation. We found an old house on a lake to rent for ten days. No TV. I was nervous about it, and this shook me. *How can you be nervous about being alone with your children?!* I decided it would be an experiment. Maybe we could live without television, just for these few days.

And we did—easily and fully. One hot afternoon I lay on a blanket under an ancient chestnut tree, idly watching the kids scramble into its massive arms. First one, then another dared to go further, and they giddily called down to their grounded Mama. Something stirred in me as I remembered what it was like to climb and climb, up and out of the reach of adults.

As I sprawled under that tree, I realized that all my best childhood memories took place outdoors. Ice skating on vacant lots in Idaho winters; huckleberry picking with a coffee can tied around my waist; racing down an alley on a summer night, pretending not to hear my mother calling me back to the house. I wanted that for my children—the endless days of girlhood and boyhood, and the time and space to make things happen. I thought about those four daily hours of television as I gazed up into the tree. I knew as the kids grew older TV would take up more of their time, would settle more firmly into our routine. Unless I did something about it.

We returned home. Without a word, I unplugged the set and placed it on the bureau in our bedroom. We filled the days emptied of Big Bird and Mr. Rogers with simple things. I dragged out the box of blocks from under the bed and asked for a city that mice could live in. I filled an apple box with art supplies—not just paper and felt-tip pens, but big-kid stuff like tape, hole punchers, and staplers. I left the box where they could reach it, not in a cupboard or closet that would require my help to retrieve it.

When the dreaded predinner hours arrived, I sent the protesting children out onto the deck with trucks and tricycles. There were days they mashed their faces pitifully against the sliding glass door calling, "What about 'Sesame Street'?" But I allowed—even invited—the boredom, that unsatisfied state of mind that drives us all to find something, *anything,* to shake it off, even if it meant throwing those same trucks and tricycles over the edge of the deck, down the ravine, to be irretrievably buried in nettles.

I have discovered over the years that I am not so much against TV as I am for honoring the spark and drive in all children that lead them to play, experiment, create, and make messes. And that takes time—the kind of time that television devours, that could be better spent riding bikes, building forts, and discovering the secret trails and haunts that make memories. TV *can* be a valuable learning tool, both in the classroom and at home. Let's face it: The growth of a seed, the habits of wildlife, and the clamor of a Moroccan market have more impact on television than when read about in a book. If television is managed, our world is widened and informed. But if television is abused, we spend our lives watching other people's adventures and ideas.

"Have your own adventures," I tell our children when they ask for more TV. They look at me sourly and roll their eyes. It seems another absurd dictum, like wearing coats in the rain or going to bed when you're not tired. But then they do go off and have their own adventures. And if they are lucky, on a hot summer day years later, they may lie under the welcoming arms of a tree and remember ...

Boxes of
Possibilities

These boxes are jumping-off places for self-discovery and hours of creative fun, and best of all, they'll generate play that is self-directed and requires no supervision. If you did nothing more than supply a few of them—an inventor's box, an art box, or a dress-up box—you would provide your family with the tools to make a thousand and one ideas happen.

Keep these resources close at hand. When a child is continually forced to ask for the tools to make an idea happen, the drive of creativity (and spontaneous fun) diminishes. Keeping the boxes accessible also frees up your time and allows your children to develop independence and self-reliance.

Carve out a space where creativity is welcome. The ideal situation is a room off the kitchen with a big old table and room enough for the boxes and supplies. If you don't have a room off the kitchen, consider placing an old table somewhere. Even if it is nothing more than a card table, it can still be the place where adults surrender the inevitable nicks and stains to the province of imagination. Not all activities create disorder, but the most satisfying ones often do.

Allow the mess that often follows creative fun. A clean house is a temporary condition; creativity lasts a lifetime.

Use boredom as an ally—it can lead to the place where ideas are born. Once your children see that you are not going to fix it for them, they have no choice but to find fun themselves. This is the same powerful skill that leads scientists, artists, and mathematicians to fool around with the ordinary and arrive at astonishing discoveries.

Puppet Box

Over the years of creating with children, I discovered that demonstrating a project often put a lid on their own unexplored ideas. When I held up my perfect model their attention seemed to slide away. It became clear that the most fulfilling creative experiences were those that gave the children the most freedom. And so we do projects informally around our house. Ideas shift and flex with the materials at hand as we estimate, snip, glue, make mistakes, backtrack and start over again. This process is difficult for an adult like me, burdened with years of "right" and "wrong" ways of making things, but effortless for children who trust their hands.

One day I put an extravaganza of materials onto a table and asked the children to make their own puppets for a show. Six boys and girls, ranging in ages from three to nine, swiftly found their own comfort level of creativity—the youngest drew eyes on an old sock while the oldest began to stuff a nylon stocking for an authentic looking face. I joined the fun in my own wobbly way. For over an hour the room was filled with the alert silence of engaged minds. The ingenious puppets created that afternoon sprang from unchecked imaginations, not the pages of a how-to book.

What you will need:

socks

white adhesive tape

toilet paper tubes

popsicle sticks or tongue depressors

small paper bags, small cereal boxes, egg cartons, small milk cartons

felt-tip pens

paper plates

styrofoam balls and cups

fabric scraps, yarn, buttons, ribbon, felt, needle and thread

corks

old nylon stockings

loose-leaf reinforcement rings

construction paper, crepe paper, poster board

pipe cleaners

walnut shells

clothespins

feathers

batting for stuffing

fingers cut from rubber and cloth gloves

Look through junk drawers and use your imagination!

Give it a try! Keep the following materials in a box and bring it out on a rainy Saturday when there's nothing to do. I have also included the instructions for three simple puppet-making projects for those who need a little guidance. When the puppets are finished, make a simple, removable puppet theater with a shower rod that screws into place in a doorway. Cover the rod with a blanket or sheet and let the show begin!

Sock Puppets

You may have to help younger children with the sewing part of these puppets, but they are simple enough for even non-sewers like me to enjoy making.

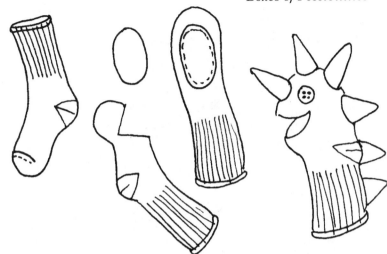

What you will need:

old socks

yarn, felt, material scraps, buttons

felt-tip pens

needle and thread

To make a mouth for the puppet, cut a slit around the front toe seam of the sock. The bigger the cut, the bigger the mouth. Cut an oval piece of felt big enough to fit into the slit, pin it into place and stitch. Turn the sock inside out. For a fancy puppet, you can sew in a tongue or scalloped teeth made from the felt.

The rest of the decorating is up to you. Use buttons or scraps of felt for the eyes and yarn for hair. A simple scarf from a square of fabric adds a nice touch, or sew on a beret circle or ears made from felt. If the sock is too big for little hands, stuff the nose and lower jaw with cotton.

Peanut Marionettes

Peanut marionettes make excellent travel or sick-bed entertainment for children. A lap or a tray is a fine stage on which to turn imaginations loose in a confined space.

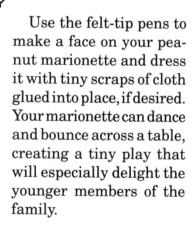

What you will need:

*bag of peanuts
(with shells)
long needle and thread
felt-tip pens*

Use a long, narrow peanut for the main body and four smaller peanuts for the arms and legs. The needle must be longer than the longest peanut.

Thread the needle, knot the thread, and run the needle from the pointed end to the rounded end of one peanut leg, then into the lower end of the long peanut and up through the head. Leave approximately 6 inches of thread and cut. Do the other leg the same way. For the arms, knot the thread and run the needle through one peanut, through the body just under the head, and into the other peanut arm. Knot the other thread end close to the peanut.

Use the felt-tip pens to make a face on your peanut marionette and dress it with tiny scraps of cloth glued into place, if desired. Your marionette can dance and bounce across a table, creating a tiny play that will especially delight the younger members of the family.

10

Finger Puppets

What you will need:

*fingers cut from small
rubber gloves* **or**

*peanut shells (Break them
in half from the middle
and remove the nut to
leave a space for a finger.)*

*fine-point permanent pen
to draw faces and bodies*

Your child can make a face and body on
the glove finger or peanut shell with the
pen and act out a story. I begin one of our
favorite finger puppet stories with: "You
think I'm little now, but I wasn't always
this way. A long time ago I was as big as
you. Let me tell you how it happened so
it will never happen to you. . . ."

Inventor's Box

There is an Inventor's Box in our garage filled with the kind of junk most people love to get rid of. Two coffee cans, a bicycle chain, an old eggbeater, and a broken thermostat from the newly repaired furnace are the latest additions. The box is used year-round and has generated everything from doll furniture to intricate contraptions that magnetically close doors.

When you clean out the garage and junk drawers to create your Inventor's Box, keep in mind that almost everything has potential for invention. Grand ideas are hidden in the pieces of an old game, the innards of small appliances, cat food cans, and rubber bands.

Most of all, remember that inventing is a process, not a product.

You may have similar invention ingredients (disguised as junk) in drawers and under beds but not collected together and *called* an "Inventor's Box." That's the secret. By placing the items into our box, the rules of function are eliminated and the bits can be reinvented into something new. Children, with their unburdened perspective, are naturally equipped to discover new uses for familiar objects.

The *act* of creating cultivates creativity in children, not the creation itself. Our spirited four-year-old reminds me of this often. He thinks invention and adventure are the same word. "This is for my wire adventure," he declared one day, holding up a trio of rusty coils. And, of course, he is right. There is little distinction between the process of inventing and the adventure of self-discovery.

Art Box

Every home needs an Art Box filled with the wondrous ingredients of creation. It cannot be replaced by an easel and some fancy paints. With simple supplies from the Art Box, my kids have made extraordinary birthday cards, festive holiday decorations, and illustrated stories. The Art Box is the most-used resource box in our home and has traveled through the years of growing children like a good friend. Keep it within easy reach and include things normally reserved for adults.

What you will need:

a ream of typing paper

felt-tip pens

stapler

hole puncher

crayons

scissors (a good pair of scissors, or your child will forever ask to borrow yours)

lots of tape: transparent, masking, duct, etc.

construction paper

plastic report covers in a variety of colors

glue stick

tissue paper

bingo markers (bright nontoxic paints with a sponge applicator— available wherever bingo is played)

Dress-Up Box

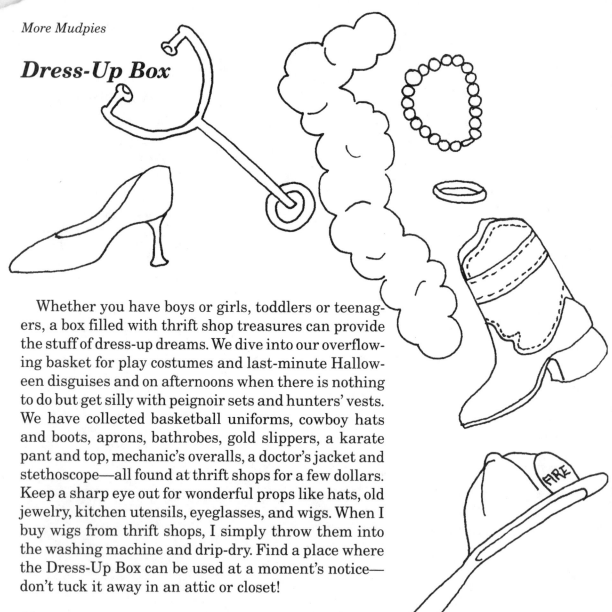

Whether you have boys or girls, toddlers or teenagers, a box filled with thrift shop treasures can provide the stuff of dress-up dreams. We dive into our overflowing basket for play costumes and last-minute Halloween disguises and on afternoons when there is nothing to do but get silly with peignoir sets and hunters' vests. We have collected basketball uniforms, cowboy hats and boots, aprons, bathrobes, gold slippers, a karate pant and top, mechanic's overalls, a doctor's jacket and stethoscope—all found at thrift shops for a few dollars. Keep a sharp eye out for wonderful props like hats, old jewelry, kitchen utensils, eyeglasses, and wigs. When I buy wigs from thrift shops, I simply throw them into the washing machine and drip-dry. Find a place where the Dress-Up Box can be used at a moment's notice— don't tuck it away in an attic or closet!

A Craft Kit for All Seasons

A Craft Kit can provide countless hours of creativity. It differs from the Art Box in the more unusual nature of its contents.

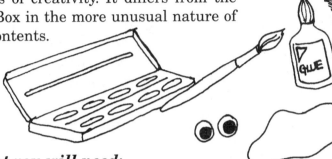

What you will need:

pipe cleaners

popsicle sticks

modeling clay

Play-Doh

utensils such as spoons, butter knives, and potato ricers

piece of linoleum to use as a work surface for clay and paints

watercolors

tempera paints

paintbrushes (lots of them, in all sizes)

copper wire or craft wire

glue

paper: butcher paper, wrapping paper, tissue paper, and so on

tape: electrical, masking, duct, transparent

paper clips and tacks

dyed feathers

doilies

aluminum foil

stamp pad and stamps (we have a whole separate bin for ours)

pieces of cardboard or old game boards

water-soluble ink and a brayer to roll in it

cotton balls and cotton swabs

Our Craft Kit, which began with a tub of home-made play dough and a few kitchen utensils, has spilled over to great bins of stuff used for creations I never could have imagined. Don't be limited (or intimidated!) by this list. Supply the items you are comfortable with, and gradually add to it with the help of your child. If you find paints too messy, keep them out of your kit. My bane is glitter, which brings on an alert vigilance that can dry up even the most imaginative project. Use your own criteria when supplying your kit and stick with it!

Outdoor Resource Box

In an ideal world, children would possess large chunks of time to spend outdoors, where nature tugs us into her realm of magic. Most children are naturally drawn to the rich invitation of ponds, vacant lots, the margins of forests and fields, or the arms of a great tree. Providing a box of tools and gardening equipment that belong only to your child will save your own equipment from the indelicate work of fort building and industrious digging. It also inspires a child to come up with a task to use these authentic tools! Equip your box by browsing at thrift shops and garage sales. As you select, consider the age and temperament of your child. All children need supervision when using unfamiliar equipment. Take a moment to demonstrate the safe and appropriate way to use the tools. Label everything with your child's name and remind her that she needs to return the tools to their box at the end of the day.

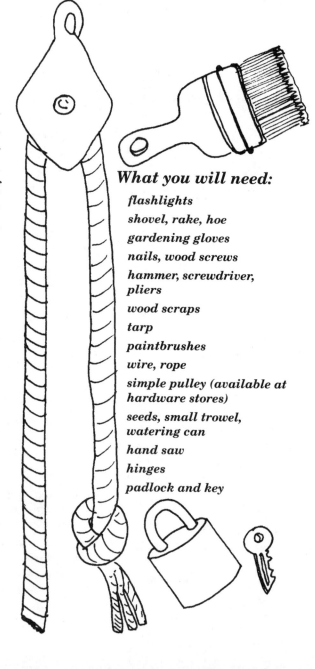

What you will need:

flashlights

shovel, rake, hoe

gardening gloves

nails, wood screws

hammer, screwdriver, pliers

wood scraps

tarp

paintbrushes

wire, rope

simple pulley (available at hardware stores)

seeds, small trowel, watering can

hand saw

hinges

padlock and key

Indoor
Alternatives

Keepsake Place Mats

It began with one crazy headline in a magazine. I had just sorted through our photographs to place in an album, and there were dozens left over that I didn't want to toss. Among the discards were several shots of the boys in a cardboard box, making villainous faces. (One picture like this is enough for any album.) Later that evening, I was idly flipping through a magazine when a headline caught my eye: "Weirdos in a Strange Land." The picture of the boys in the box surfaced. I smiled, got a pair of scissors, and cut the line out. Several pages later: "I Have Three Brothers." Daughter Jenna can relate to the impact of that small statement. I cut that one out, too.

Out of an amusing diversion, the seeds of an idea were planted: I would make place mats for the kids and surprise them. I soon had a growing pile of headlines to accompany not only the discards but also other shots that were especially personal: Jenna on her horse, Ben boogie boarding, Nick and Daniel fishing.

TOXIC WASTE SITE DECLARED ELIGIBLE FOR SUPERFUND MONEY

GIRL SAYS HORSE WAS GEORGE WASHINGTON IN PREVIOUS LIFE

I cut forest green poster board into an approximately 12-inch by 20-inch rectangle. At the top of each child's mat I placed huge cut out letters of their names. After trimming the photographs, I arranged them along with the relevant headlines on the poster board. The headlines are what makes these mats so distinctive (and such outrageous fun!). A glue stick works beautifully to hold everything in place. To finish the mats, I used adhesive plastic laminate (available on a roll) found at our local office supply shop, and I carefully wrapped each mat, front and back, leaving a half-inch overlap all around to seal it.

How to describe the enraptured faces of my children when they discovered their gifts at breakfast one morning? It's been over a year, and they still pore over every silly detail. This project has become an ongoing event around our house. We now keep a file for amusing headlines, not only to record changing interests and growing selves, but as a daily reminder of the special people that share our lives.

Art Mural

You don't need to be famous artists to make this mural an extraordinary work of art. Best of all, this is a collective painting the whole family works on.

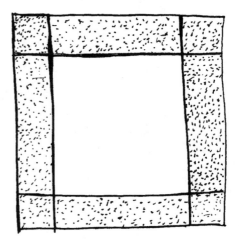

Frame the canvas with the duct tape around the edges to provide an unpainted outline to highlight your work, then divide the canvas into sections with the tape. This allows each artist his own space and eliminates the worry of slopping paint into the margins of the mural.

Give each artist a section of the canvas to work in. Think of a theme or allow family members their own subjects. Our three-year-old was happy brushing big stripes in his section, while our nine-year-old painted an elaborate horse scene.

When all the sections are finished, let the paint dry, then gently lift the tape from the canvas. The clean edges between each painting gives the canvas a wonderful "professional" look. You can choose to create a pattern in the margin or leave it unpainted.

What you will need:

large- or medium-sized canvas (inexpensive and available at art supply stores and most variety stores)

tempera or poster paints

paintbrushes in a variety of widths

duct tape or similar tape to divide the canvas into sections

Love Medicine

We were at the zoo one day when I paused to read the display on the lions dozing before us. It mentioned the enormous amount of time lions spend collectively napping, playing, and grooming one another. It is a survival mechanism called "pride time," and it keeps the lions bonded and functioning as a unit. I left the display reflecting on the lack of "pride time" in our own family. We were all simply too busy to nap together or scratch backs or lazily sprawl on a blanket in the sun. And yet it is often the smallest of gestures—a careful hair brushing, eye contact when listening—that speak the loudest of love. "Love Medicine" is a project to help remind us of the importance of small gestures.

What you will need:

large empty capsules (the kind real medicine comes in—available at your pharmacy)

slips of paper to fit inside medicine bottle

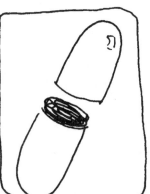 

Ideas for medicine:

Good for breakfast in bed

You deserve a foot rub!

Pick a book to read together

Let's go for a walk

Play Blind Man's Bluff (our version is to take turns leading a blindfolded person around the house or outside)

Good for 14 kisses in a row

Go out for breakfast Saturday morning alone with Mom or Dad

A nice long back scratching session is in order

Let's play the card or board game of your choice

Good for cookies and milk in bed

Get out the bubble gum! Let's see who can blow the biggest bubble

Teach Mom or Dad something you have learned recently

See if Mom can still lift you with her legs into the air six times

Let's all make peanut butter and jam sandwiches blindfolded

Skip a chore for today

Your choice for dinner tonight and you can help make it

Use the list below or dream up your own medicine with your family. The messages can be handwritten, or if you have a computer, print using a small font size. Cut each message out and roll it up tightly to fit inside the capsule. Make a bright Love Medicine label and write out the directions:

To be used as needed for rotten days, too much homework, and stubbed toes. Keep out of reach of mean people.

Ma-Jean's Magic Jar

It was my idea of a great rummage sale. I skipped the tables with crowds around them and headed for the empty corners where creative possibilities lay disguised as junk. I found old transistor radios and alarm clocks for the kids to take apart, horn-rim glasses and a scatty wig for the dress-up box, a tin of colored thread on wooden spools, and best of all, a large cardboard box of ancient Coleman parts (valves, screens, springs, and brass coils) just waiting for the uninhibited to reinvent the lantern.

On my way to the cashier, I cast one last glance over the toy table when an old peanut butter jar caught my eye. Curious, I pulled it out from between the piles of games and books and read the label: "Ma-Jean's Magic Jar (For times when the kids say there is nothing to do but watch TV)." Inside were orange slips of paper. I unscrewed the lid and pulled one out. "Make a house! Use chairs, couch cushions, blankets." I added the jar to my pile of treasures.

Later that night I read the rest of the slips. "Have a picnic on the front porch." "Pretend you fell down and bumped your head and broke your leg. Grandma can be the doctor." "Have a parade with records." The slips went on to suggest that making Jell-O, writing letters, and turning seven somersaults were all a lot more fun than watching TV.

Try some Ma-Jean Magic. Sit down with your children and fill the jar together. Ask them what they consider fun. Add your own ideas. Some of our favorite things to do are as simple as reading a book together or making pancakes in the middle of the day.

The shared pool of suggestions makes this project a success. They are not vague orders from an adult, like "Go outside and play," but instead offer immediate and tangible alternatives a child helped think of himself.

Handmade Musical Instruments

These simple instruments are as much fun to make as they are to play! They can also be used for sound effects when recording stories or plays on cassette tape. Keep in mind that your children can invent their own musical instruments using the materials listed below.

What you will need:

1-inch-thick dowel, sold in 4-foot lengths at hardware stores

saw

sandpaper

paints or felt-tip pens to decorate

Rhythm Sticks

Rhythm sticks have ancient roots in musical history. Even this simple version yields a rich, woody tone to set the beat of your band.

If your child can handle a saw, let her saw the dowel into 1-foot lengths. Then she can sand the rough edges and decorate the sticks with the paints or felt-tip pens. Encourage your child to experiment with different rhythms by tapping the sticks lightly together. Think syncopation and play along with a pair yourself!

Bell Bracelets

What you will need:

*small jingle bells, sold at
fabric and craft shops*

pipe cleaners

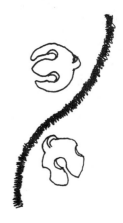

I use pipe cleaners instead of string for these bracelets to ensure versatility (you can take the bracelet off and hold it like a tambourine) and ease (even a three-year-old can thread the bells onto a fuzzy wire). Simply string the bells onto the pipe cleaner and twist the ends together to make a bracelet. Your child can shake his wrist or tie the bracelet around an ankle for music made from dancing feet!

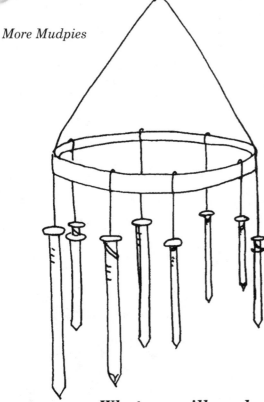

What you will need:

small embroidery hoop (a stick or a canning jar ring will work fine, too)

large nails of various sizes

fishing line, or light- weight string

Nail Chimes

These hanging nails produce clear, ringing tones, and choosing them from the hardware store's bins with your child is half the fun! The size of the nail determines the tone of the chime. Experiment!

Cut a length of fishing line, tie one end under the head of the nail, and secure the other end to the embroidery hoop. Continue tying the nails around the hoop at more or less regular inter- vals until the frame is full. When fin- ished, strike the nails gently against one another for bell-like chords, or hang the nail chimes outdoors and let the wind make your music.

Water Drum

Water drums, with their special resonance, stir up wonderful images of shamans and ceremony. You can make a drumhead out of a less expensive material than chamois (such as canvas or heavy plastic), but the effect will not be quite the same.

Fill the pail one-fourth full of water. Stretch the chamois over the mouth of the pail or can, and bind tightly into place with the twine or wire. The drumhead needs to be as taut as possible for the full sound effect. You can also tape the chamois into place with duct tape, but it is more trouble to remove when storing the drum.

If the chamois seems a little loose, wetting it inside and out with the water will cause the skin to shrink and tighten when it dries. Use bare hands to play, or if drumsticks seem important to your child, try a pair of chopsticks.

What you will need:

tin pail or coffee can— different sizes will produce different sounds

chamois (enough to cover the top of the pail with at least a 1-inch overhang)

twine or thin wire

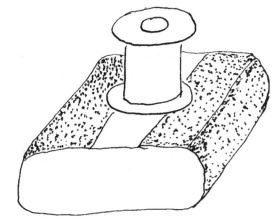

Sandpaper Blocks

Children love the scratchy scuffle of these blocks. Make two pairs from different grades of sandpaper, rub them together in any combination, and compare the change in sounds.

What you will need:

4 small blocks of wood

2 grades of sandpaper (a coarse grade and a finer grade)

thumbtacks

2 empty thread spools and 2 nails for handles, if desired

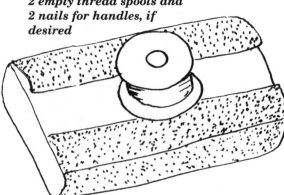

Have your child wrap the sandpaper around a block of wood as if she were wrapping a present. Don't worry about tidy corners. Or cut a strip of sandpaper the width of the block and forget about wrapping the sides. Either way works fine. Use thumbtacks to hold the paper around the block, and finally, nail on a spool if you want a handle. Make another sandpaper block the same way so that you'll have a pair to rub rhythmically together.

Swap Shops

Swap shops are not only great fun, but also they build organizational skills and foster cooperation among children. They also strengthen the idea that everyone has something to offer.

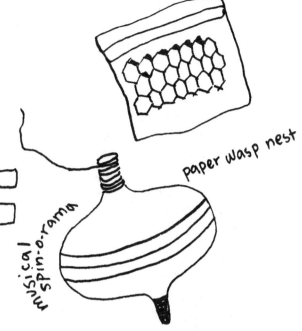

paper wasp nest

musical spin-o-rama

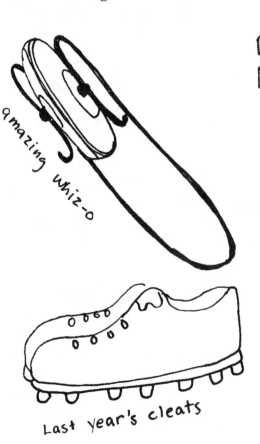

amazing whiz-o

Last year's cleats

Introduce the idea to your child and encourage him to clean out closets, cupboards, drawers, and toy boxes to come up with items to be traded. Invite your child's friends to bring their treasures and set them up. All trades are mutual undertakings, and the process (left to the children) of determining a fair swap will help ease their territorial preoccupation with forgotten or discarded toys.

Old-Fashioned Taffy Pull

It takes only an hour—from cooking to cleanup—to make a wonderful memory on a winter evening. My kids were shocked that normal human beings could actually make such wonderful stuff. ("Don't machines make this?") Yet taffy is incredibly simple, and pulling it is great fun for all ages.

What you will need:

1 cup sugar

¾ cup light corn syrup

⅔ cup water

1 tablespoon cornstarch

2 tablespoons butter

1 teaspoon salt

2 teaspoons vanilla

candy thermometer (optional)

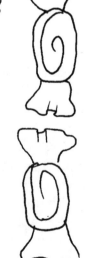

Mix all the ingredients except the vanilla in a medium-sized saucepan. Stir over medium heat until it begins to boil. Insert a candy thermometer into the cooking taffy and stir occasionally until it reaches 250 degrees Fahrenheit. If you don't have a thermometer, cook the taffy until a small amount dropped into cold water forms a hard ball. Remove from the heat and stir in the vanilla.

Butter a cookie sheet. When the taffy has reached the hard ball stage, pour it onto the cookie sheet. Turn the edges into the center as it cools, and when it is cool enough to handle, butter your hands and let the fun begin! Cut off pieces for everyone, and pull and twist the taffy until it changes color and becomes satiny. We found that if we stretched the taffy without breaking it and then doubled it back upon itself for another pull, it was easier to form it into strips after it cooled. Use scissors to cut the pulled taffy into one-inch pieces and wrap them in waxed paper.

Family Cookbook

Some of the best family memories and traditions have their roots in food. Everyone has a favorite meal, a cookie recipe, or a dish that represents the good things in life. Collecting them together in a book can preserve these cherished recipes and offer even the youngest a voice in family history (she may know the best way to make a peanut butter sandwich!). Consider a chapter on fast meals or favorite things to put in school lunches. If your child is particular about food, she may want a chapter entirely to herself on the kind of food she enjoys and how to prepare it. Ask relatives to contribute their favorite recipes with a brief account of who likes it best and how it arrived in the recipe box. Add to the cookbook as the years go by. It will make a priceless gift when grown children are ready to be launched into the world.

After-School Snacks Kids Can Make

Children who learn to cook are apprenticing themselves to a dying art. It seems few people these days have time to spend in the kitchen. I, like most of my friends, learned from watching my mother. My mother kept the refrigerator filled, tried out the latest casseroles, and taught me how to make a perfect pie crust. I've never appreciated my mother's culinary skills as much as I do today, as I pass them on to my own children.

My children's participation often means a disorderly kitchen, a sticky floor, and extra dishes, but it is worth the extra time and trouble, because they love it. They love to sink their hands into dough or stir a bubbling pot. They love to knead and blend and measure and peel. And I find that if I have the right attitude, if I can surrender to the clamor and mess, then I am passing on more than culinary skills—I am passing on the ancient love of nourishment.

After school is a fine time for children to try their hand with this gentle art. Many of the following recipes can be made with little or no supervision; others may require your help. Either way, remember that the kitchen, no matter how messy, can always be cleaned up. And in time, they will learn to clean up after themselves.

Fruit Kabobs

Whether fruit kabobs are eaten as an after-school snack or as part of a meal, they are a fun and nutritious way to eat fruit.

What you will need:

> *bamboo skewers*
>
> *grapes (washed and pulled off the stems)*
>
> *bananas (sliced)*
>
> *can of pineapple chunks (drained)*
>
> *cantaloupe or honeydew melon (scoop out pieces with a melon baller)*

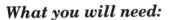

Fast Pizza

This was one of the first snacks my children learned to make.

What you will need:

> *English muffin*
>
> *tomato paste*
>
> *grated cheddar cheese*

Spread the muffin with tomato paste. Top it with cheese and broil until bubbly.

Place each kind of fruit in a separate bowl. Push the pieces onto a bamboo skewer in repeating patterns.

Indoor S'mores

This project is simple with a micro-wave oven. If you don't have one, you may need to help your child melt the chocolate chips in a double boiler.

What you will need:

2 inner packets of graham crackers

jar of marshmallow creme

2 cups chocolate chips

wire rack

Break the graham crackers into the quarters marked on the cracker; this is a good size to work with. For an easy cleanup, place a piece of waxed paper under the wire rack to catch chocolate drips. Ready to make S'mores? Generously spread the marshmallow creme on one of the quarters and place another quarter on top to make a sandwich.

Melt the chocolate chips in the micro-wave oven for 1½ minutes on high power. Stir them, and if they are not completely melted, microwave them again for 30 seconds. If you are using a double boiler, melt the chips over boiling water. Stir until all the chips are melted.

Dip the graham cracker sandwich in the melted chocolate and coat both sides. Place on a wire rack to set. Yum!

Melt Art

Indoor voice zone
no yelling
in this area

What you will need:

electric warming tray or griddle (keep your eyes open at garage sales)

crayons

typing paper

watercolor paints (optional)

This is one of those projects to which words cannot do justice. Children of all ages love it! If you are using an electric griddle instead of a warming tray, tape the temperature setting into place as low as possible. Then, if there are any bumps, the temperature setting will be secure.

Turn the griddle or warming tray to a low temperature and let it heat up. Place a piece of paper over the warm surface and color with the crayons. The crayons melt into beautiful, dense colors that have the look of an exotic paint.

Our family had a great time making a series of panels to tape around the house, telling people to wash their hands, warning boys to lift the lid, and requesting visitors to take off their shoes before coming into the house. After each message or drawing was finished on the griddle, we painted over it with watercolors. The wax resisted the paint and gave the panel a lovely finished look.

Bird Feeders

Birds contribute a great deal to the underlying framework of our world. For example, many species have remarkable appetites for the insects that damage food crops. They also limit the spread of weed seeds.

The winter months are a good time to introduce your family to the wide variety of birds that live in your area. Your kids can create simple feeders and a smorgasbord of gourmet bird treats. Not only will the birds appreciate the diversity in their diet, but your family will learn more about this group of animals and its importance for the environment.

Keep in mind the following ideas for your feeder station:

• Recycle your Christmas tree by placing it outdoors and hanging the feeder(s) from its branches during the slow months after the holidays.

• Your local library or bookstore should have books that will help identify birds that visit your station. The Audubon Society's *Field Guide to North American Birds* is an excellent one.

• If a visiting bird hits your window and is stunned, gently place it in a shoe box lined with a soft material and cover the box with a cloth. Set the box in a dark place until the bird recovers.

Plastic Jug Feeder

What you will need:
  plastic jug with lid
  scissors
  twine
  fat nail and hammer
  electrical tape

Rinse the jug thoroughly and drain. Cut several windows in the jug big enough to allow a bird to perch on the edge and feed on the seed you will be placing in the bottom. Cover the edges of the windows with electrical tape or sand them with sandpaper until smooth and blunt.

To make a hanger for your feeder, drive a fat nail through the cap of the jug and thread a loop of twine through the hole. Knot the end of the loop to secure in the cap. Fill the feeder with birdseed or your homemade recipes and add a rock for stability and balance.

Pinecone Feeder

Tie thin wire or string around a pinecone and butter its "petals" with a heavy layer of peanut butter. Roll it in birdseed and hang it up.

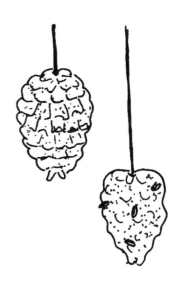

Corn-on-the-Cob Feeder

Hammer several long nails into a small board to form spikes to hold the cobs of corn. The nails should be spaced widely enough to allow birds easy access around the cobs. These corn feeders will also attract grain-feeding game birds such as quail and pheasant, if there are any in your area.

Doughnut Feeder

This simple feeder appeals to children as well as birds—better make several! Hammer a nail through a metal jar lid to make a hole for threading heavy string. Do the same to another lid. Then thread a lid onto a piece of knotted twine or string, add a doughnut, and thread the other lid on top of the doughnut. Tie your doughnut feeder to the branches of a tree.

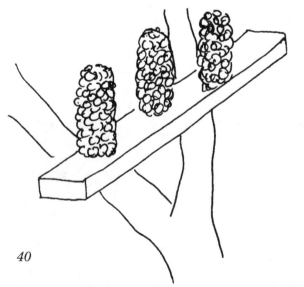

Gourmet Bird Treats

The following ingredients will allow your children to invent their own nourishing bird treats without the imposing instructions of regular food recipes. Provide any or all of the dry ingredients, along with a bowl for each participant. Bind the loose ingredients with the peanut butter or the suet melted in a pan on the stove. Our family enjoyed using paper cupcake holders to make "muffins" or "cupcakes." You can also shape the finished recipe into cookies, balls, or bars, or leave the seeds loose to fill a feeder.

sunflower seeds

commercial birdseed

nuts

dry dog food crumbs

raisins

bread crumbs

unsweetened dry cereal, such as puffed rice or shredded wheat

cornmeal

oranges cut into small pieces

a pinch of clean sand for the grit birds need

corn, dry or fresh

popcorn

peanut butter

beef suet (available in the meat department of your grocery store)

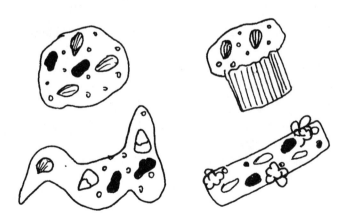

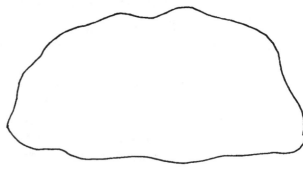

What you will need:

1 cup peanut butter

1 cup nonfat dry milk

⅔ cup powdered sugar

1 loose cup of coconut, if desired

eat a goober duck

Edible Modeling Dough

What better after-school project than one you can not only play with, but eat? Older children can make it themselves if the ingredients are handy.

Place the peanut butter in a big bowl and work in the nonfat dry milk with your fingers. Children love to help with this. Add the powdered sugar and the coconut, and continue to work it all in with your fingers until it is incorporated. The dough should have a Play-Doh-like consistency. Add more peanut butter if it seems too dry or powdered milk if too sticky. This mixture keeps well for a week in a plastic bag in the refrigerator.

Puffy Paint Jewelry

We were all surprised at how reward-ing it was to create puffy paint jewelry and how beautiful it turned out. The process is simple, relatively clean, and the children—including all of the kids on the block—enjoyed every minute of it. Many thanks to our neighbor Mary McCormic for the inspiration!

Even though this project is amazingly mess-free, it is a good idea to lay news-paper over your work area to catch extra drips from the paint. Give each child a plastic plate to work on, provide the paints, and let them go! You can make specific shapes such as hearts, stars, or fish, or you can freely color within the boundaries of the plate and cut out a shape after the paint has dried (about four hours).

Cut the painted forms from the plate (you may want to cut it wide for colorful margins). For a necklace, you can use a hole puncher to make a hole and hang it from a colored cord. To make smaller

What you will need:

fabric puffy paints

plastic disposable plates in primary colors

colored cord or thread for necklaces

earring hangers or posts for earrings (available at hobby stores and some fabric stores)

pin backs (available at craft or hobby stores) or safety pins

holes for earrings, heat a needle over a flame for a moment and gently push it through the shape. Thread the earring hanger through the hole. We found that a hot glue gun works best to secure an earring post to the back of the form. A hot glue gun also works for securing the pin back or safety pin to the painted shape to make a brooch. Be careful not to touch the hot tip of the glue gun directly to the plastic plate, or it may melt.

Holiday Art

Handmade Gifts for Any Occasion

There is no better way to teach children the fine art of gift-giving than allowing them to make the gifts themselves and participate in something more meaningful than a quick trip to the mall to fulfill holiday obligations. Take your time with these projects; deadlines can take the pleasure out of creativity.

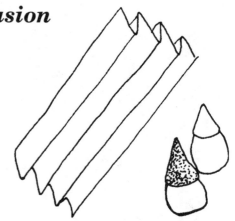

Dip-Dyed Tablecloth

If you choose only one gift-making project during the holidays, make it this one! The process is a rewarding one and offers participants the chance to play with color. Best of all, when the pieces are taped together it makes a truly spectacular gift.

The secret for vivid colors in your tablecloth is a high concentration of food coloring in the water. Squirt at least a teaspoon of each color into separate containers and add approximately half a cup of water to each container.

There are many ways to prepare the paper towel for dipping. One is to fold the towel into a fan and then fold the length of *that* piece, fanlike, into a small square packet.

With the towel folded, you are ready to dye it. Hold the packet firmly, and *briefly* dip each corner into a different color dye.

What you will need:

plain white paper towels (2-ply works best)

food coloring

water

newspapers

colored masking tape, sometimes called "painter's tape" (available at hardware or building supply stores)

If you soak up too much food coloring, the colors will be muddy looking. Unfold carefully and lay it on spread-out newspapers, or if you have the space, string some yarn for a temporary clothesline for drying. Experiment with different ways of folding for a variety of patterns. We even dip-dyed a paper towel folded into something like an airplane and came up with a beautiful pattern.

When all your pieces are dry, iron them smooth with a fairly hot iron. This step gives the towels a fabriclike texture by strengthening and joining the fibers.

To put the tablecloth together, lay the ironed pieces out on the floor (six down and five across is a good size), and tape the corners together with a bit of cellophane tape. This holds the pieces in place for the next step, outlining with the colored masking tape.

The outlining is a two-person job. Have your helper hold one end of the masking tape while you pull it out into long strips to lay upon the seams of all the towels, across and down, until they are all outlined. Now, stand back and behold this beautiful piece of art!

Handmade Gift Wrap

These easy stamps add a special touch to every wrapped gift.

What you will need:

1 or 2 packages of adhesive-backed latex foot padding, available at your pharmacy (used to protect feet from shoes that rub)

small blocks of wood

scissors

tempera paint (felt-tip pens or a stamp pad will also work)

colored tissue paper or plain brown mailing paper

Cut a simple design or holiday symbol from the foot padding. Remove the paper from the adhesive side and stick it onto the block of wood. To print, dip the stamp into a small dish of paint (scrape the excess drips off), and press the stamp onto your wrapping paper. You can also rub a felt-tip pen over the entire surface and get a great color transfer. Gold tempera paint on purple tissue paper looks magnificent.

Hand-Stamped Apron

After we made this apron for a teacher, I had to have one for myself! A single-color fabric paint looks fabulous on a bright color. Try yellow hands on a red apron or blue hands on a green one.

Before you begin, wash the aprons to remove the starch (the paint will adhere better), then iron the apron smooth. Squirt a small amount of paint onto a damp sponge and gently rub it over your child's palm. Have her press her hand onto the apron. Repeat over the entire apron. After the paint has dried, iron over the hands to help set the paint.

What you will need:

plain, bright-colored apron (inexpensive and available in a wide range of colors at import stores such as Pier One)

acrylic paint

sponge

iron-on letters for child's name (optional)

Super-Easy Marbleized Postcards

This is a simple version of marbleized paper, using spray-on enamel paint. I use big index cards because the enamel makes writing on the marbleized side difficult if you run out of room.

What you will need:

enamel spray paint

large index cards

foil-covered cookie sheet with rims, or a tray

Spread newspapers over your work area. Fill the cookie sheet halfway with water, then shake up a can of spray paint. Spray the surface of water lightly with the paint and swirl with a stick to create a pattern. Lay an index card onto the surface and lift—a beautiful design in seconds!

What you will need:

bleach

cotton swabs

colored tissue paper (many shops sell a brilliant array of colors by the sheet)

newspaper

Batik Bleach Art

Batik bleach art is astonishingly simple for people of any age, and the results are glorious. Young children should be supervised with the bleach and reminded that stray drips may take the color out of clothing.

Cut the tissue paper into a workable size and lay a piece on a newspaper. Pour a little bleach in a bowl and add a tiny bit of water (not too much!). The rest is simple. Dip a cotton swab into the bleach mixture and "paint" a picture on the tissue. The bleach removes the color from the tissue, giving it a rich batik look. For a finer stroke, use old paintbrushes.

Handmade Cookie Stamp

 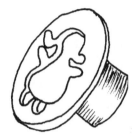

What you will need:

Fimo or Sculpey clay (clay that hardens in the oven)

popsicle sticks, pencils, or any item that will make an impression or give texture to the clay

Put your children to work before the holidays begin by having them make their own cookie presses! It's a fun way to add a special touch to gifts of homemade cookies. The cookie stamps themselves also make unique gifts.

Break off a piece of clay the size of a walnut and work with it until it is soft enough to flatten smoothly into a cookie-sized circle. Use the popsicle stick or pencil to press a design firmly into the clay. Bake the stamp according to the directions on the clay package.

When it is ready, spray the stamp with nonstick spray and flour it. Roll your cookie dough into a walnut-sized circle and gently push the stamp over it. We found that shortbread-type recipes (or those with little or no baking powder) work best with these stamps, leaving the image intact. Cookies that rise and spread tend to obliterate the picture.

YOUR BIRTHDAY FORTUNE: HIRE THE NEXT CURLY-HORNED YAK THAT AS YOU FOR A JOB!

Paper Tube Surprises

Paper tube gifts have always been a hit for us. After school, have your child prepare these for a party (they make great favors) or for gifts to give during the holidays. They can be decorated as simply as a tube covered with stickers or as elaborately as an angel with cotton hair.

Decorate the tube with imagination as your guide, then tape one end closed. Fill with the selected treasures, then tape the other end closed. The ends can be covered with construction paper cones or fringed tissue paper, if desired.

What you will need:

paper tubes from toilet paper or paper towels

decorating materials: construction paper, tissue paper, felt-tip pens, stickers, pipe cleaners, gift wrap, colored cellophane, cotton, and so on

bingo markers (bright, nontoxic markers with a sponge applicator, available wherever bingo is played)

They are optional for this project, but I urge parents to have them on hand as a valuable addition to your child's art supplies.

tape

small gifts to stuff the tubes with: candies, bath oil beads, marbles, coins, erasers, Legos, rubber stamps, costume jewelry, chocolate coins, a packet of seeds—anything that will fit

Simple Candy Cane Ornaments

These ornaments are easy enough for a three-year-old to make and clever enough to satisfy the older members of your family.

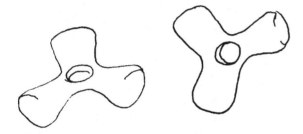

Make a tiny hook at the end of a pipe cleaner to secure the beads, then thread them onto the pipe cleaner. Bend the finished pipe cleaner into a candy cane and hang on your tree.

What you will need:

pipe cleaners

tri-beads in red and white (Tri-beads have three sides that fit snugly on top of each other. Available at craft and hobby stores.)

Autumn Celebrations

Jack-O'-Lantern Totem Pole

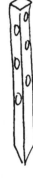

These totem poles are a wonderful way to display Halloween pumpkins, particularly if you have an enthusiastic child who wants to carve a dozen of them! (Children who are too young to use sharp knives and matches can help stack the pumpkins.)

Decide where you want to place your totem pole and drive the fence post into the ground up to the crossbar. Make a small slit with a sharp knife at the bottom of the biggest pumpkin. Slip it over the post and add a candle inside. Place the rest of the

What you will need:

several carved pumpkins

votive candles

metal fence post (Fence posts are inexpensive at feed stores or hardware stores. Ask if they also have a "slammer" you can borrow—a device that drives the post into the ground easily.)

jack-o'-lanterns, from biggest to smallest, up the totem pole (without their lids), adding candles as you go. You may have to trim the openings here and there to level each pumpkin.

When dusk arrives, light your jack-o'-lanterns. Have a helper lift the upper pumpkins and using a long match, light the candles inside. Last year, we put a totem pole on both sides of our driveway for a wonderful port of entry for trick-or-treaters.

Homemade Face Paint

Children love helping to create this versatile makeup. Experiment with the food coloring to come up with the perfect camouflage green or monster purple.

Mash the shortening and cornstarch together with a fork in a shallow bowl or saucer until well mixed. If you want another color besides white, divide the paste and add a few drops of food coloring until it reaches the desired intensity. Refrigerated, this recipe will keep for a week.

What you will need:

1 tablespoon vegetable shortening

2 tablespoons cornstarch

food coloring

Pumpkin Candy Carrier

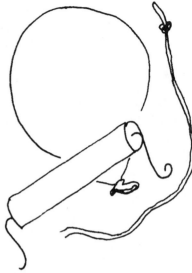

Papier-mâché is a little messy, but don't let that stop you. It is simple, and children love it. Dive in with your kids and make a holder for the house candy.

To make the papier-mâché paste, mix the flour, sugar, and alum in a saucepan. Slowly add one cup of the water and stir out all the lumps. Bring the mixture to a boil over medium heat, stirring constantly. Remove from the heat when smooth and clear and add the remaining ¾ cup of water. The paste can be made several days ahead of time if kept in a sealed container in the refrigerator.

When you are ready to make the carrier, spread newspapers over your work area and lay out the supplies: a blown balloon for each carrier, newspaper strips, and the paste in a wide, shallow bowl (you may have to thin the paste with a little water for easy spreading).

What you will need:

For the paste:
¼ cup flour
¼ cup sugar
½ teaspoon alum
1¾ cup water

For each carrier:
round balloon blown up and tied
strips of newspaper, 2 inches wide
plastic hand holders from a shopping bag or sturdy twine
poster paint

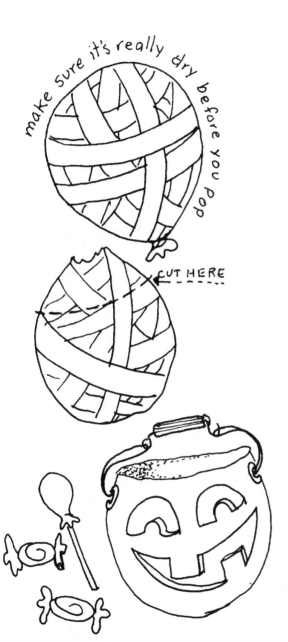

make sure it's really dry before you pop

CUT HERE

Cover the balloon with paste-covered newspaper strips in crisscrossed layers for strength. Children have a tendency to overdo the paste, but let them. After the strips are laid, you can show them how to smooth out the wrinkles and spread the excess paste a little more evenly.

Leave a small opening near the top of the balloon and lay extra layers of newspaper strips around it for reinforcement—this is where the handles will be punched through and taped. After two or three overall layers, place the balloon in a warm, airy place to dry. It may take several days, depending on how much paste is used and how humid the weather is.

Now for the best part: Pop the balloon! (If the papier-mâché is not completely dry, the carrier will cave in.) Trim the opening, then paint on a jack-o'-lantern or other design. (Spray paint provides a fast, fun way to cover it, too!) When the paint is dry, punch holes for the twine or plastic handles and secure with lots of tape. The handles should be secure enough to hold lots of candy!

Winter Celebrations

Apple Candelabra

As the darkening of the winter season approaches, light up your life with candles! This project makes a great group activity during holiday parties, in classrooms, or at Scout meetings.

You may want to try the pyramid shape below, but the apples and evergreen look splendid in any form. The chopsticks provide a sturdy base. Experiment!

To make a pyramid-shaped candelabra, connect three apples into a triangle with three of the chopsticks. Next, angle a chopstick upwards from each apple to poke into the remaining apple. You now should have a three-dimensional pyramid.

Wire the mixed greens around the chopsticks to cover, then place a candle into each apple near the stem. You may want to carve out a bit of apple to allow the candle to fit more securely.

What you will need:

4 apples

mixed greens such as evergreen and holly (perhaps your yard has shrubs that will work)

6 chopsticks or sturdy sticks

florist or craft wire

4 candles (chime candles—the small candles used in revolving candle centerpieces—work best)

What you will need:

thin wire (available at hardware stores or florists)
cranberries

Cranberry Wreath Ornaments

Decorate your tree with these colorful ornaments, or add a special touch to your gifts with cranberry wreaths tied to the bows.

Cut a piece of wire long enough to curve around into an 8- to 10-inch circle. Pinch an end of the wire into a small loop; this will secure the berries and provide a means to tie off the wreath when filled. String the cranberries onto the wire, leaving enough wire to string through the loop at the end. Secure and snip off the overlap.

Clothespin Star Ornaments

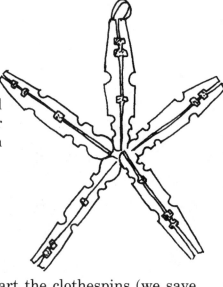

The first time I saw these beautiful ornaments, I was amazed to discover they were made with nothing more than ordinary clothespins!

What you will need:

package of wooden clothespins (the type with pins, not pegs)

glue, or better yet, a hot glue gun
(Although hot glue guns require adult supervision, they are perfect for this project.)

ribbon

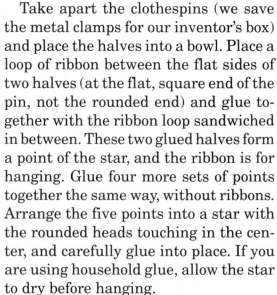

Take apart the clothespins (we save the metal clamps for our inventor's box) and place the halves into a bowl. Place a loop of ribbon between the flat sides of two halves (at the flat, square end of the pin, not the rounded end) and glue together with the ribbon loop sandwiched in between. These two glued halves form a point of the star, and the ribbon is for hanging. Glue four more sets of points together the same way, without ribbons. Arrange the five points into a star with the rounded heads touching in the center, and carefully glue into place. If you are using household glue, allow the star to dry before hanging.

Sculpted Ice Candle

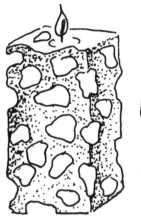

Try this easy way to make a truly special candle.

To make the mold for this beautiful candle, cut the milk carton a few inches above the height of the old candle you will be using. Place a wad of clay in the bottom and lower the old candle into place.

To melt the paraffin, place 2 or 3 inches of water in the larger can and lower the smaller can with the paraffin into it. Bring the water to a boil over medium-high heat. Just before the wax is completely melted, add a crayon for color, stir with a chopstick to dissolve, and remove from the heat.

Place the crushed ice around the candle secured in the milk carton, then carefully pour in the paraffin. The wax will harden around the ice, creating weird and wonderful spaces. Allow the wax to cool, then pour off the water from the melted ice. Peel away the milk carton and behold your unique candle!

What you will need:

1 package paraffin (available in the canning section of the grocery store)

2 empty cans for melting wax (we use one large coffee can and one small)

crayon

ice, crushed into small pieces

quart-sized milk carton

old candle

Play-Doh or clay

Floating Walnut Candles

Make this project a holiday tradition in your home. Children love the big, soft light these tiny candles give off. Float a number of them in a glass bowl of water for an unusual centerpiece, or if you dare, float them in the bath at night (with adult supervision, of course).

The trickiest part of this project is cracking open the walnut shells into undamaged halves. Try placing a walnut in a hand-held nutcracker with the seams aligned with the bars of the cracker (small end of the nut facing in). Pick out the meat and any remaining inner shell.

Line the cookie sheet with foil or paper towels and anchor each walnut shell half with a small piece of clay onto the cookie sheet.

Melt the paraffin in a modified double boiler by pouring 2 or 3 inches of water into the large can and lowering the small can containing the paraffin into the water. Heat over medium-high heat on the stove. Just before the paraffin is all melted, add a crayon of your color choice to the wax, stir with a chopstick to dissolve, and remove from the heat.

Carefully dip a piece of cotton string, a few inches long, into the melted paraffin, remove, and set aside. Then spoon the melted wax into a walnut shell and allow to cool slightly (a skin may begin to form). Place the wax-dipped string into the center of the shell. You may have to hold the string there for a moment to keep it centered until the wax hardens enough to secure it. When the wax has cooled, your floating candle is ready!

What you will need:

walnut shell halves

paraffin (available in the canning section of the grocery store)

crayons

cotton string or candle wick from a candle supply store

two empty cans for melting the wax (we use one large coffee can and one small)

cookie sheet

Play-Doh or clay

Festive Table Runner

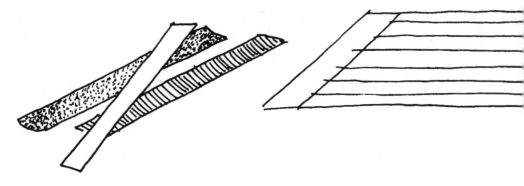

What you will need:

foil gift wrap (red or green looks great for the season)

strips to weave: construction paper, ribbon, lace, aluminum foil, yarn, gift wrap, colored cellophane, and so on

glue

clear contact paper (optional)

This project should be done in a slow and leisurely way. We let ours sit on the kitchen table for days, and as people gathered to visit or rest at the table, they contributed by weaving some of the strips. It became a rich tapestry of many hands that not only looked wonderful, but also symbolized the collective spirit of the holiday season.

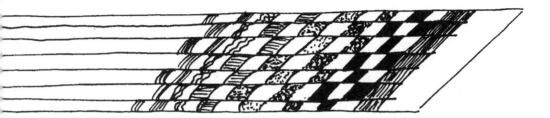

I found it was easiest to prepare the foil gift wrap and the strips myself before calling in the troops for action.

Cut a long rectangle from the foil gift wrap to the length and width you want your table runner. I usually place a sheet of clear contact paper on the reverse side for strength and durability, but this step isn't necessary. Eyeball the width of the runner and cut your weaving strips to overlap both ends.

Next, cut lines the length of the runner approximately 1 to 2 inches apart, leaving a wide (2 to 3 inches) uncut band at both ends to hold the runner together. Now you are ready to weave! Remember to weave the strips in an alternating pattern as you go. A spot of glue or tape at the ends of the strips will also help to hold them in place. With a smaller version of this project, you can make wonderful place mats, too!

Spring Celebrations

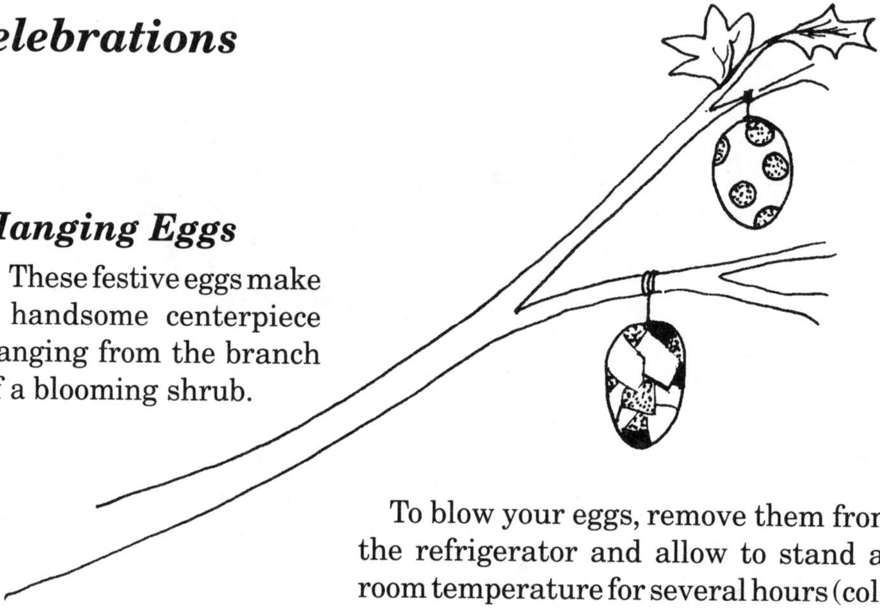

Hanging Eggs

These festive eggs make a handsome centerpiece hanging from the branch of a blooming shrub.

What you will need:

*blown eggs
(directions follow)*

cotton swabs

*brightly colored tissue
paper cut into small
shapes*

white glue

wooden matchsticks

colored thread

To blow your eggs, remove them from the refrigerator and allow to stand at room temperature for several hours (cold eggs are more difficult to blow). Use a darning needle or a hat pin to pierce a hole about the size of a nail head in the large end of the egg. Make a smaller hole at the other end. Have your child blow the contents of the egg into a bowl from the smaller hole. It may be a little difficult at first, but have patience—this is great fun. Rinse the eggs and let them dry.

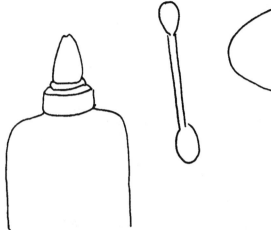

To hang an egg, tie a length of thread to a small wooden matchstick; to secure it, touch the place where it is tied with a spot of glue. When the glue is dry, carefully insert the matchstick into the largest hole of the egg. The stick will become wedged crosswise into the egg and hold it for hanging.

You can hang these bright eggs from a round wooden embroidery hoop, a piece of driftwood from the beach, or a small branch spray painted with a contrasting color. They also look wonderful hanging in a window. If you want to keep the eggs year-round, spray them with a fixative or paint them with clear nail polish.

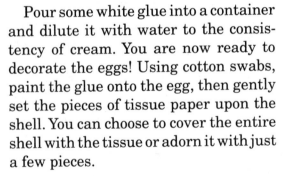

Pour some white glue into a container and dilute it with water to the consistency of cream. You are now ready to decorate the eggs! Using cotton swabs, paint the glue onto the egg, then gently set the pieces of tissue paper upon the shell. You can choose to cover the entire shell with the tissue or adorn it with just a few pieces.

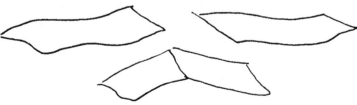

Harry in a Half Shell

If this project is started several weeks before Easter, the "hair" will have grown nice and long.

Mix the potting soil with enough water to hold it together in clumps. Place the egg shell halves into an egg carton. Gently pat the soil into each shell and top with a light sprinkling of grass seed. Keep the soil moist over the course of the next few weeks, until the seed germinates.

After the seed has sprouted, draw faces onto the shell with the felt-tip pens and use the growing grass for hair—give it a Mohawk, or tie on tiny ribbons to create pigtails. After Easter, use the eggs for a hands-on science lesson. Remove a clump of grass and point out the complex root system to your child. Note the fine root hairs and the way roots shape themselves to the container. Then plant the clump in a bald spot on your lawn!

What you will need:

egg shell halves saved from breakfast

potting soil

grass seed

felt-tip pens

Green Grass Easter Basket

This is a great alternative to plastic grass for filling Easter baskets. Start early enough for the grass seed to germinate and thicken in time for Easter.

What you will need:

basket

plastic garbage bag or plastic wrap

potting soil

grass seed (available in small quantities at nurseries and hardware stores)

peat moss (optional)

Cut the garbage bag into a piece large enough to cover the inside of the basket. In a large bowl or bucket, mix the potting soil with water to dampen. You may also mix peat moss with the soil to help retain water as the grass grows.

Spoon the damp soil into the basket. You need only a couple of inches. Just be sure there is an overhang of plastic; you can trim it after the grass has grown.

Sprinkle the seeds on top of the soil in a thin layer. To hasten germination, place the baskets in a warm, well-lit place and keep the soil damp with daily misting or gentle watering. The grass seeds will sprout anywhere from a few days to a week later.

Chocolate-Covered Easter Eggs

This project is a wonderful way for families to spend an afternoon. The recipe is delicious, simple, fast, and fun. The peanut butter center is easy to shape, and the colored foil wrappers give the eggs a special touch. This batch makes enough for four children and two adults to play with. Give some away to neighbors and friends, then make more for yourselves!

What you will need:

1 cup peanut butter

1 cup nonfat dry milk

⅔ cup powdered sugar

1 loose cup coconut, if desired

12-ounce package of semisweet chocolate chips

foil candy wrappers (available at craft stores that carry cake and candy supplies and at some candy shops)

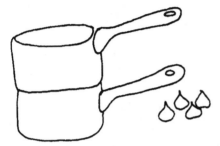
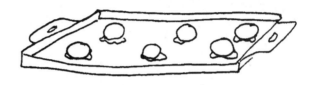

Place the peanut butter in a big bowl and work in the nonfat dry milk with your fingers. Children love to help with this. Add the powdered sugar and the coconut and continue to work it all in with your fingers until it is incorporated. The dough should have a Play-Doh-like consistency. Add more peanut butter if it seems too dry or powdered milk if it's too sticky.

Shape pieces of the dough into eggs (or stars or balls). Now you're ready for dipping. Melt the chocolate chips in the microwave following the manufacturer's directions or in a double boiler. We started out very neatly toothpicking our creations into the melted chocolate, but soon abandoned that method for the more sensible (and fun!) finger method. Lay the dipped eggs on a cookie sheet covered with waxed paper. When the chocolate hardens, the eggs are ready to wrap in the foil wrappers. Enjoy!

May Day Basket

What you will need:

This recipe will make one medium-sized or two small baskets

1 cup salt

1½ cups hot water

4 cups white flour

ovenproof bowl or casserole dish to use as a form

aluminum foil

1 egg beaten with 1 teaspoon water

Don't let May Day slip by this year. Pass on the wonderful tradition of giving flower-filled May baskets in secret. Even if it is simply dandelions in a paper cone for a neighbor or a teacher, celebrate the coming of summer with others!

I was reluctant to try this salt dough basket with my family—it was so attractive I felt sure the process would be tedious. To our surprise, it was fun and easy, and a treasure to give away. All the weaving is done on a flat surface and then lifted onto the form, making it easy even for little ones.

Pour the salt into a medium-sized bowl and add the hot water. Stir until the salt partly dissolves (it will not dissolve completely). Allow to cool, then add one cup of flour and stir until all the lumps are worked out. Add the rest of the flour one cup at a time, stirring well after each addition. Knead the dough until smooth and pliable. If the dough seems too sticky, add a little more flour; if too dry, add a few drops of water.

Take ¾ of the dough and roll it out on a lightly floured surface until it is about ⅛ of an inch thick (slightly thinner than rolled out Christmas cookies).

Next, place the ovenproof bowl or form upside down on the table. Press a square of aluminum foil over it and trace the bowl's rim with a permanent marker. Smooth the foil flat again on the table top. The marked area indicates how long your dough strips need to be. Cut 1-inch-wide strips from the rolled dough.

Now weave the lattice of your basket. Lay strips in a row on the outlined shape on the foil, approximately ¾ inch apart. Trim where necessary. Weave dough strips in the opposite direction in an over-and-under pattern (don't stretch the dough as you weave). Work your way across the form until the lattice pattern is complete.

Turn the baking dish upside down on a cookie sheet. Lift the foil with the lattice and carefully place it on top of the baking dish. Tuck the excess foil inside the dish, then gently press the dough lattice onto the form with your hands.

To make an edge for the basket, take the leftover dough and divide it into two pieces. Roll each piece into a snake long enough to wrap around the lip of the basket. Wind the snake pieces together to form a twist. Wet the dough ends at the edge of the basket and press the twist into them. Bake the basket at 300 degrees Fahrenheit for 30 minutes, then gently remove the basket from the dish by pulling up the edges of foil. Turn the basket over into an upright position, remove the foil, and brush on the egg and water mixture, inside and out (this gives the basket a rich, golden brown color). Return to the oven and bake another 15 minutes. Remove and cool completely on a wire rack.

When May Day arrives, tie on a bright ribbon handle and fill the basket with fresh flowers!

Keep It
Simple

Bead Bucket

One of the most used treasures around our house is a bucket filled with beads. The bead bucket began with the wild and colorful beads of several necklaces I no longer wore. I had put the necklaces in a box aimed for the thrift shop when my daughter spotted them and said she could make a truly beautiful bracelet out of them. I snipped the string, emptied the beads into a bucket, and that was the start of many beautiful bracelets and many hours of creative fun.

Stringing beads is a satisfying way for children to spend time—the task has a beginning and an end, with a wonderful creation to show for their efforts. I particularly love this activity because it keeps those frisky hands and minds happily occupied when I am trying to complete my own tasks.

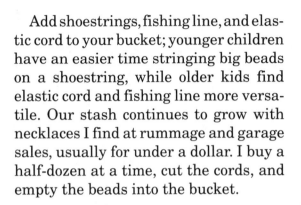

Add shoestrings, fishing line, and elastic cord to your bucket; younger children have an easier time stringing big beads on a shoestring, while older kids find elastic cord and fishing line more versatile. Our stash continues to grow with necklaces I find at rummage and garage sales, usually for under a dollar. I buy a half-dozen at a time, cut the cords, and empty the beads into the bucket.

The creative possibilities are endless. Both girls and boys enjoy creating jewelry such as earrings and necklaces (great gifts for Grandmother!) and enjoy inventing toys, such as popsicle-stick cars with beads for wheels and glued-together bead creatures. Don't wait for a trip to a specialty bead shop; stop at a local thrift shop or neighborhood garage sale and buy your family the seeds of imagination!

Greeting Card Cut-Outs

One wise grandma once sent a box of old Christmas cards to her granddaughter who was traveling by plane with her mother for a visit. The five-year-old spent the entire four-hour flight happily cutting and taping the pieces of cards to paper. This activity can also be effective for sick days or for the times you need a quiet but amusing diversion for your child.

Save old greeting cards, birthday cards, and special stamps cut from envelopes and put them in a shoe box along with blank paper (large blank postcards work great, too), scissors, and a glue stick or transparent tape. Pull out the box and ask for "new" cards from the old.

Magnet Maze

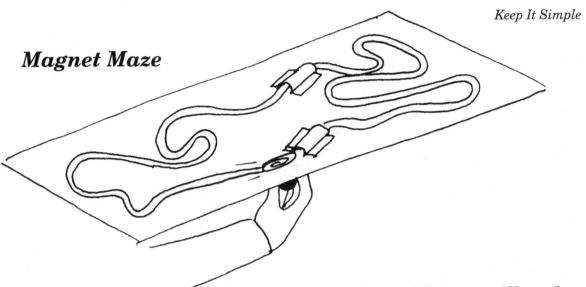

Kids of all ages enjoy this activity. Younger children will find tracing a squiggly line with their paper clip challenging enough, while the older ones love to try their hand at designing a maze (astonishingly difficult!).

It's simple. Have your child draw a maze or a line on the poster board with a felt-tip pen. Place the magnet under the paper and a paper clip on top, then draw the paper clip along the path or lines by moving the magnet. You can pretend the clip is a fish trying to find food or create a story with your child as the magnet travels across the page.

What you will need:

small magnet (very inexpensive at hardware stores)

small piece of poster board or a paper plate

paper clip or small metal washer

optional: *a small box or sealable bag labeled "magnet experiment," containing small objects your child can experiment with to discover which are attracted to a magnet*

Cardboard Weaving

This is a good lap activity for rainy days or sick days.

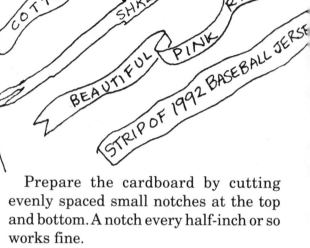

COTTON T-SHIRT FROM DISNEYLA

SHREDED PLASTIC BAG

BEAUTIFUL PINK RIBBON

STRIP OF 1992 BASEBALL JERSE

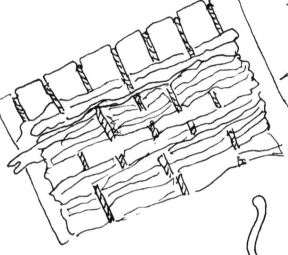

What you will need:

small piece of cardboard

pieces of yarn, ribbon, or fabric strips in a variety of colors

Prepare the cardboard by cutting evenly spaced small notches at the top and bottom. A notch every half-inch or so works fine.

Warp (string) the cardboard by tying or knotting the yarn around the first notch and running it up and down the notches on the face of the card only. When ready to weave, run pieces of yarn in an in-and-out pattern between the warped string and pull the weaving down to the bottom of the cardboard with fingers. Your child can work out the best manner of weaving for himself. Even if the weaving pattern is loose or imperfect, he will be proud of his efforts.

Island Hippety-Hop

Oh, how my children enjoyed this crazy little game when they were toddlers! Even now, they find it great fun on a rainy day. It is simple. Take all the cushions off the sofa, chairs, beds, and benches. Lay them out on the floor within jumping distance from each other, and tell your child that the floor is water and the pillows are the safe islands to land on. (For a fiercer version, our boys liked to imagine the floor was hot lava.)

Spin-a-Word Spool

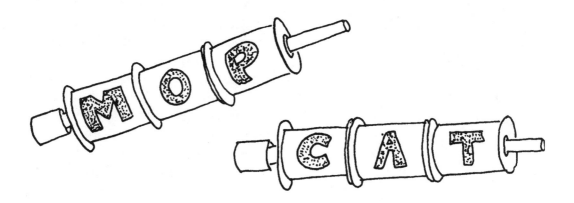

I was surprised at how much my children loved playing with this simple contraption. Although it is especially effective for prereaders and those beginning to learn the alphabet, my 11-year-old daughter was eager to make her own and invent word games. You can also use numbers instead of letters for simple math problems.

Ask your child to pick out four consonants from the letter pack and place them around the first spool. Then ask for four vowels for the second spool and another four consonants for the third spool. The first time we did this, I encouraged letter combinations for the spools that would spin up familiar words like "m-a-d" or "c-a-t."

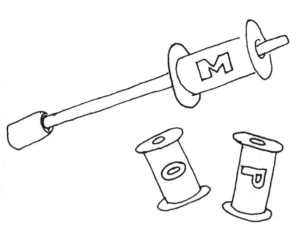

What you will need:

3 empty sewing thread spools
(Large white ones work best. Make sure the center hole is big enough for a pencil or chopstick to fit through.)

unsharpened pencil or chopstick

adhesive letters or numbers, ½ inch or larger (you can also write them on, but these give a clearer, bolder look)

duct tape or masking tape

Wrap tape around one end of each pencil or chopstick to make it thick enough to keep the spools from sliding off. Thread on the first spool, the vowel spool, and the second consonant spool. Tape the other end. You are ready to spin up your words! The spools spin freely, permitting your child to come up with many different words.

Glass Art

What you will need:

inexpensive picture frame with glass (any size will work)

permanent markers in a variety of colors

Using glass as your medium provides an interesting experience for your child and a beautiful piece of art for you!

Carefully remove the glass from the frame and have your child clean it with window cleaner. Lay the glass on a piece of newspaper and let your child draw directly on it with the permanent markers. She can use her imagination or trace over a favorite photograph or picture. Our son lay the glass over a photograph and traced his favorite baseball player. (Tracing is more appealing to older children and perfectionists, and the effect is just as wonderful.)

When the art is finished, cut a piece of construction paper to fit behind the glass and provide a colorful contrast to the picture. I used our preschooler's purplish finger painting for the background of a horse scene: it gives an impression of an impending thunderstorm. Slip the glass picture back into the frame with the contrasting mat, and voilà! A framed picture to make any artist proud!

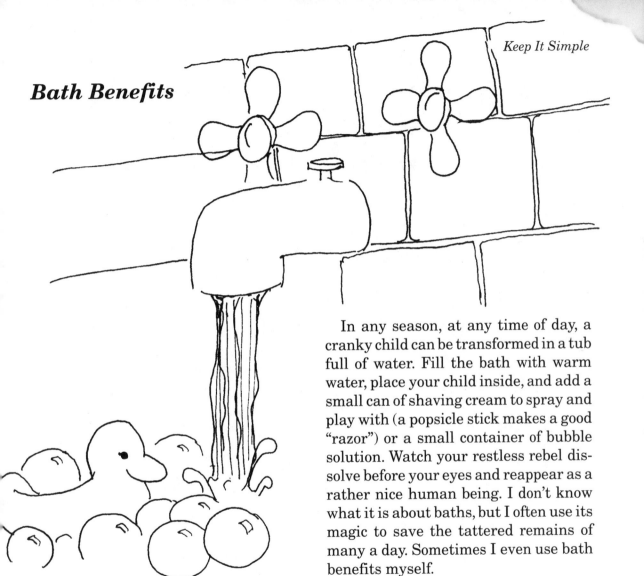

Bath Benefits

In any season, at any time of day, a cranky child can be transformed in a tub full of water. Fill the bath with warm water, place your child inside, and add a small can of shaving cream to spray and play with (a popsicle stick makes a good "razor") or a small container of bubble solution. Watch your restless rebel dissolve before your eyes and reappear as a rather nice human being. I don't know what it is about baths, but I often use its magic to save the tattered remains of many a day. Sometimes I even use bath benefits myself.

Any-Age Art Activity

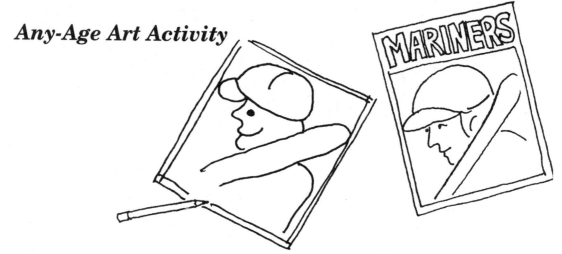

Tracing pictures may sound a little dull, but children love it! It also develops the fine motor skills that are necessary for younger children to learn to write. Be sure to let your child help pick out the pictures to trace. Her own taste should take precedence over a parent's selection; it increases her willingness to invest time and energy in tracing them.

What you will need:

tracing paper

pictures to trace (simple cardboard-page picture books are good or magazine pictures of a special interest your child may have—baseball, wild animals, horses, trains)

fine-point felt-tip pens or pencils

Time for Memories

My children grow instantly alert at the words "When I was a girl. . . ." I tell them of the indignities I suffered, the adventures I had, the bullies I escaped, and the tree forts I built. It is hard to imagine a parent as a kid, but it helps both to find common ground. Remote parents are brought down to earth and are made more accessible, and parents recapture the child inside. Take the time to pass your memories on—in a grocery store line, while cooking dinner, before bedtime, or when your child is restless while waiting for something. We all have stories to tell.

Vegetable Soup

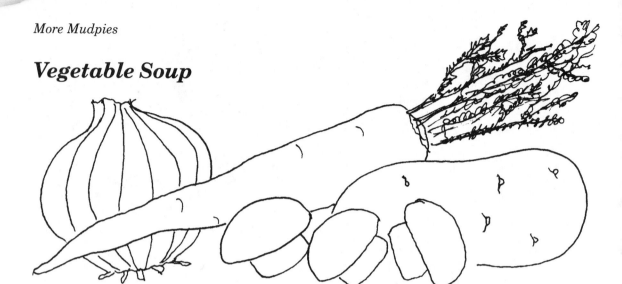

I cannot tell you how many times this simple activity has saved me when I needed some time to prepare a meal or pick up the house. One day there were some carrots sitting on the counter, and my son asked if he could make a soup with them. Well, one thing led to another, and before I knew it, he had a pot of carrots, onions, and potatoes simmering on the stove. A cut-up apple was thrown in for good measure. It smelled good, tasted OK, and was a rewarding way for us all to spend the afternoon.

The kids have invented many pots of soup over the years, experimenting with different herbs (add, taste, add a bit more) and additions of pasta and rice. Some soups were more successful than others, but the secret to this activity is to allow your child artistic and culinary freedom. Place the ingredients on the table with a knife (you may need to supervise). Include herbs and spices, water or chicken broth, and a nice big pot. You may or may not enjoy the fruits of your child's labor, but it is the process of discovery that matters.

Dictionary Game

panegyric- someone who goes crazy at a party and dances with pans between their teeth -Mel

Panegyric-the physical forces that separate planets and keep them from falling off course-Al

Whether you play this game in a large group or just with your own family on a rainy afternoon, I guarantee some good laughs. All you need is a dictionary, paper, and pencils. The object of the game is to guess the definition of an obscure word no one has heard of before.

Pass out paper and a pencil to everyone participating. Have someone find a word in the dictionary that no one knows the meaning of (even in a group of adults, this is strikingly easy!). Then each participant creates a definition of his own and writes it down on the paper while the person with the dictionary writes down the real definition. Pass all the definitions to the dictionary person, and then he reads them all out loud to be voted upon. The person who guesses correctly picks the next word from the dictionary.

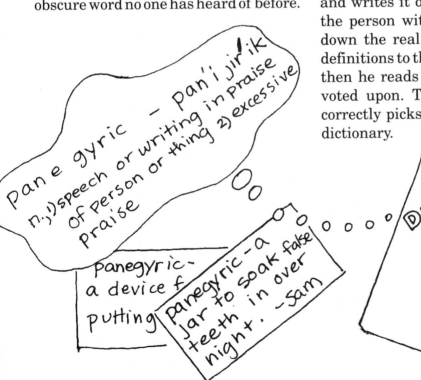

Pan e gyric — pan'i jir'ik n.) speech or writing in praise of person or thing 2) excessive praise

panegyric- a device f putting

panegyric-a jar to soak fake teeth in over night. -Sam

89

King or Queen for a Day

WARNING: MAKE SURE YOU TELL ALL CUPCAKE EATERS TO WATCH FOR THE BEAN

QUEEN

BEAN ROY

ROYAL ORDERS
CHOICE OF CAR
RADIO STATION
∞
SUBJECTS MUST
CLEAN MY ROOM
∞
ADDRESS ME AS
"YOUR LOVELINESS"
∞
I GET 4 DESSERT
PORTIONS

There is nothing so fine as being treated like royalty for one day. You can skip chores, decide what to eat for dinner, and map out an afternoon of *your* kind of fun. The rules for selecting the first king or queen for the day are simple. Make a cake and drop an uncooked bean into the batter (cupcakes work well, too). When the cake is served, the person with the bean is Queen or King for a day. (You may want to make a few rules beforehand to determine the limits of royal power!)

Reading Aloud

Most parents recognize the academic importance of reading aloud to children, but what isn't considered often enough is the warm and inviting climate a good book can generate. In our family, bad days are often redeemed through the continuing adventures of our latest protagonist. We have a wide range of ages to consider—from 6 to 12, so I look for books that tell a good story simply. Don't underestimate young children. A great book can be riveting without pictures, particularly if it is written in a straightforward manner. Choose a time for reading aloud every day and stick with it. For us it is bedtime. Reading aloud at night offers us the chance to unwind and fall into imaginary worlds. More important, it gives the day closure.

Following is a list of our favorite books, only a few of the thousands of wonderful books available!

The Saga of Erik the Viking, **Terry Jones**

Harry's Mad, **Dick King Smith**

The Indian in the Cupboard series, **Lynne Reid Banks**

The Fairy Rebel, **Lynne Reid Banks**

The Jack Tales: Folk Tales from the Southern Appalachians, **Richard Chase**

The Chronicles of Narnia, **C. S. Lewis**

Dominic, **William Steig** *(We'll read anything by this author!)*

My Side of the Mountain **and its sequel,** *The Other Side of the Mountain,* **Jean Craighead**

Hercules, **Bernard Evslin**

The Education of Little Tree, **Forrest Carter**

The Iceberg Hermit, **Arthur Roth**

My Father's Dragon series, **Ruth Gannet Stiles**

Island of the Blue Dolphins, **Scott O'Dell**

Discover Science

Three-year-old Heather is in the backyard on a sunny afternoon with a pan full of bubbles. Slapping the solution with a big strainer, she watches as the bubbles slosh and spill and diminish in size. "Mommy! Baby bubbles!" she crows. This is a lesson in physics.

Patrick is in the kitchen helping to make bread. He stirs the yeast carefully into warm water and waits for it to rise up the glass bowl like an unearthly potion. This is a lesson in biology.

The Potter children grow fat sugar pumpkins in their garden every year for autumn pies. This year they planted a variety of gourds near the pumpkin patch and the vines of both plants twined together companionably. When harvest time arrived, the pumpkins were smaller than usual. Many were covered with the distinctive bumps of gourds and their skins were impenetrable. This is a lesson in botany.

Science is everywhere—in the backyard, in the kitchen, at our very fingertips. For most children, however, the designated arena for science education is the classroom, a place where overloaded teachers hurry through textbook programs, where the hands-on approach is considered a time-consuming luxury. Parents can help fill in the gap by remembering one simple but powerful concept: *Science is merely a way of looking at the world*. A way of asking questions. A way of noting differences.

Young children are natural observers and collectors; their questions guide them when their minds are ready to assimilate information. A two-year-old, for example, is not ready for an explanation on electrical circuits, whereas an adolescent is equipped to test that information and apply it to other concepts. Age appropriate experiments done in the home can strengthen new concepts in lasting and far-reaching ways.

Jean Piaget, the noted Swiss psychologist, studied children's learning behavior and identified the development of human intelligence in four stages. These four stages are a helpful guide to parents and educators for age-appropriate experiments.

The Sensori-Motor Stage (birth to 18 months)

At birth, babies are governed by reflexes such as sucking and crying to insure their survival. As they move through the sensori-motor stage, babies coordinate the active use of their senses with developing motor skills to assimilate information.

At approximately 12 to 18 months, a child begins to experiment with her environment in earnest. Still dependent on direct experience for assimilating and accommodating information, a toddler's mantra at this stage is "What will happen if . . . ?" Roll balls together. At bathtime, provide your toddler with a variety of plastic containers to fill and empty. By the time a child completes the sensori-motor stage, she will be able to test the possibilities mentally. Your scientist is unfolding her wings.

The Pre-Operational Stage (Ages 2 to 7)

Experiments for two- to seven-year-olds should allow a child to use all five senses. Strengths at this stage include observing, communicating, comparing, and organizing material things. Collections are a natural inclination. Your child can gather seeds from the various plants in your area, from weeds to pine trees. Insects, leaves, rocks, and shells can be grouped by color, shape, or form.

With a magnet, a child can strengthen categorizing skills by gathering different household objects to determine which will be drawn to the magnet and which will not. Another easy categorizing project requires only a tub of water and small household items to separate the "sinkers" from the "floaters."

A collection of simple objects to take apart and put back together offers a close examination of the way things work. Flashlights with batteries, hooks and latches, and a padlock and key are a few examples.

Logical Operation Stage (Ages 7 to 12)

Seven- to 12-year-olds are capable of coordinating more than one thought when they experience new information. A child of this age can grasp complex concepts such as expansion, evaporation, and adaptation in animals and can associate or combine this information with several variables.

It is most effective at this stage of development to work with a general principle and explore it with different projects. Osmosis can be demonstrated by soaking raisins or potato slices, for example, in containers of fresh water and salt water. Seeds grown both in the dark and in a sunny location will prove that green plants need light to grow.

At the logical operations stage, the child will be able to relate a learned principle to other areas of life. The more opportunities she has to explore a single idea, the greater her understanding will be.

Formal Operations Stage (Ages 12 to 18)

From about the age of 12 through adolescence, children are capable of theorizing about a given principle. Their knowledge is not dependent upon direct experience, and they can make valid predictions about what may happen in an experiment when dealing with a new principle.

Experiments involving electricity, for example, can be more detailed and complicated than at other stages. *How can we lower our electrical bill?* Children at this stage can organize energy consumption information from several of your household appliances (refrigerator, dryer, and so on) to calculate and compare the energy consumption. Or working with a principle like friction can lead your child to examine the things that depend on friction to work, such as tires, shoe soles, brakes, or Velcro fasteners, and determine how these devices can be made more efficient.

⤳

Keep in mind that Piaget's stages are broad generalizations; there can be wide individual differences. Some eight-year-olds are as capable as a 15-year-old when it comes to creative problem solving. Don't be afraid to challenge your child with a more involved experiment than he may be capable of fully understanding.

Libraries and bookstores have many excellent books to help make your home science experiments a success. Also consider the following: *(1) It is helpful to explore one broad topic at a time: the earth, living things, the heavens, and matter and energy are a few examples.* If you have children in different academic stages, these topics can be explored with a variety of projects that will enhance and complement each child's understanding. *(2) Do not tell your child the outcome of the project.* If you allow him to make the discoveries himself, the results will have a greater impact on his understanding. *(3) Allow your child the freedom to explore further with the materials of the experiment, even if it seems redundant or foolish to you.* Encourage curiosity. *(4) Set up a regular time for experiments.* Stick with it. Even if it is only twice a month, science experiments are powerful tools for learning more about the world around us. *(5) Don't be inhibited by your own lack of science education.* In many ways, you are in a better position than people with strong scientific backgrounds because you are freer to learn like a child, to bump and roll along, make mistakes, and ask questions. You can be a powerful role model for demonstrating that learning never ends and that the world is an endless source of wonder at any age.

Color Magic

This project is full of hidden science! The pieces of colored plastic from report covers allow children to play informally with primary colors and discover for themselves the combinations that make up the hues of their world.

Cut the report covers into squares about the size of your child's hand. Ask your child to combine and overlap the pieces to come up with the color green, purple, or orange, for example.

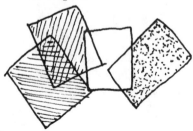

For more fun, demonstrate some magic with a secret message card. Write a message on a piece of white typing paper with the orange pen. When the message is covered with the red piece of plastic, it disappears because our eyes are not sensitive enough to distinguish the orange light coming through the red plastic. We can perceive only the red. Perhaps another kind of animal with sharper eyes would be able to read the message we humans cannot!

Invent a game with the secret message project above, pulling the red plastic aside and allowing the orange letter to show with a correct letter guess until the word or message is decoded.

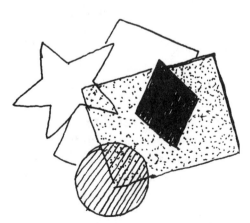

What you will need:

clear plastic report covers in red, blue, and yellow (available at office supply stores or wherever school supplies are sold)

typing paper

tape

orange felt-tip pen

Motor Activities

These motors have a small bit that spins when connected to a battery. The creative and inventive possibilities are endless! Be sure to buy several motors to keep at home for year-round fun.

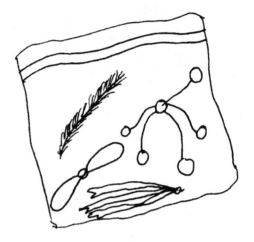

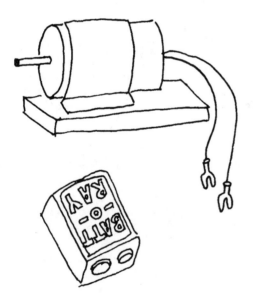

I've always taken a laissez-faire approach with children and creative endeavors, and this project is no exception. The kids soon figured out how to attach the wires to the battery and motor and get the thing running without my help. In order to write about this project, I actually had to ask my six-year-old how to do it! If your child is not old enough to figure it out, you can attach one wire to the positive terminal of the battery (the top with the nub), tape it into place, and tape the other wire to the negative terminal (the flat bottom of the battery). Then attach the wires onto the brass holders on top of the motor. The bit should spin.

With the bag of materials, your child can make a fan, a helicopter propeller, a "drill bit" made of aluminum foil, or a moving ribbon mobile. Use your imagination!

What you will need:

1.5-volt motors (available at Radio Shack or similar stores)

battery (the size of a flashlight battery or smaller)

2 pieces of copper wire

electrical tape

a small Ziploc plastic bag containing aluminum foil, construction paper, balsa wood (available at hardware stores in small amounts), small pieces of styrofoam, pieces of ribbon—anything your child might want to attach to the spinning bit

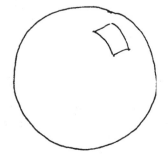

Science in the Tub

The following science projects help to take the holiness out of science. It is hard to be stiff and serious (as we sometimes imagine science to be) in the bathtub! The projects are particularly interesting for preschoolers, who may look at the results more as magic than as science. But remember, science *is* magic, with an explanation attached.

Bubble Fun

There is science in the outrageous fun of blowing bubbles! Warn very young children that the bubble solution is meant for blowing and not drinking!

What you will need:

6 cups cold water

¼ cup glycerin (available at pharmacies)

2 cups clear liquid dish soap (Dawn and Joy work best)

straws

paper cups

Mix the water, dish soap, and glycerin into an empty container and stir gently. Provide your child with a straw and have him practice blowing without sucking. Give him a cup of solution and tell him to blow with the straw into the cup. Observe the bubbles together. What happens if you blow soft? Hard? What shape are the bubbles? What happens if you insert the straw into a bubble itself and blow? What happens when a bubble lands on the water? Your skin? A hard surface such as the tub? These are the kinds of questions scientists ask when doing research.

The Way of Water

This project provided endless entertainment at bathtime in our house! It is a wonderful example of how science can be both fun and educational.

(Depending on the size of funnel, you may need ½-inch or 1-inch tubing. The best way to get a good fit is to buy the funnels at the hardware store at the same time as the plastic tubing, or bring funnels with you and fit the tubing directly onto them.)

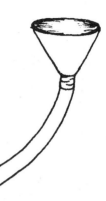

What you will need:

2 funnels (the most effective are the clear plastic ones)

3 feet of flexible plastic tubing (available at hardware stores)

Fit the tubing onto the funnels and let the fun begin! Have your child fill the funnels with water and raise and lower first one side then another. Ask her to try and make the water even in both funnels. What position are the funnels in?

What happens? The water races down into the lowest funnel. Water always attempts to level itself. When you drink a glass of water and all the water rushes to one side, it is actually the glass itself that changes, not the water. The same concept is at work in the funnels. The water seems to move but it is really the funnels that change postion.

Underwater Observation

What you will need:

large disposable plastic cup or 1-liter plastic bottle

plastic wrap

rubber band

objects to observe under water, such as small toys or rocks

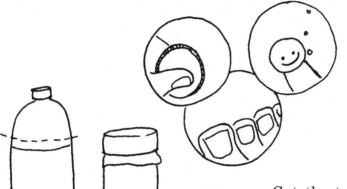

This handmade tool provides an effective means for observing things under water. Use this magnifier year-round at ponds and tide pools for a closer look at the wonderful world beneath the water's surface.

Cut the top third from the plastic bottle, then cut out the bottom, leaving a clear cylinder. If you are using a plastic cup, cut the bottom off of the cup. Take a piece of clear plastic wrap and use the rubber band to secure it around an end of the cylinder. First have your child observe the objects under water without the magnifier. Then use the magnifier to examine the objects.

What happens? The pressure of the water pushing into the wrap forms a concave magnifying lens that enlarges the objects you are looking at. Although you can see objects in the water without the magnifier, using it enables you to observe more closely.

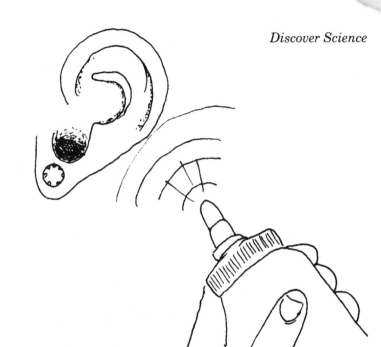

Sounds of Science

Here is a project that demonstrates the way water amplifies sound. You can also remind your child that whales and other sea creatures communicate very effectively under water because of this interesting concept.

Listen to the objects above water first and tap the pairs of different objects together. Next have your child squeeze the air out of the squeeze bottle. Listen closely to the sounds that each object makes. Now try the same thing under water.

What happens? The sounds are louder under water than in the air, because water amplifies the sounds.

What you will need:

2 wooden spoons

2 metal spoons

plastic squeeze bottle (the type that holds mustard or catsup)

2 golf balls

2 rocks

Body Science

These science projects explore the biology of being human—from our five senses to our lung capacity.

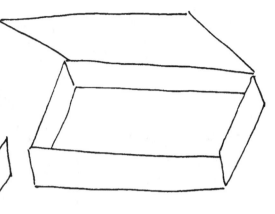

Sound Pictures

This project demonstrates how sound can guide our visual picture of the world.

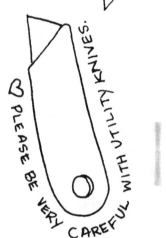

PLEASE BE VERY CAREFUL WITH UTILITY KNIVES.

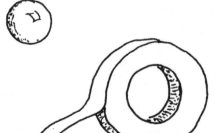

What you will need:

3 or 4 school boxes (the cigar-box-type used for pencils)

cardboard pieces (poster board works fine)

utility knife or scissors for cutting cardboard

1 marble for each box

tape

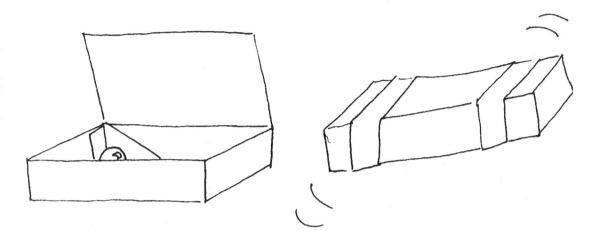

Each school box needs a differently placed cardboard insert inside the box. Measure the inside of a box diagonally to start, and cut a piece of cardboard to fit snugly on the diagonal. Measure the next box across the width and place the partition down the middle of the box, taping the cardboard securely into place. The third box can have the cardboard insert along its length. Use your imagination in placing the inserts. Any shape will work as long as it is not too intricate.

Number each box and note the shape of the partition inside. Place a marble inside each box and tape it closed. Now you are ready to test someone! Have the person draw three rectangles on a piece of paper. Hand her a box and ask her to guess the angle of the cardboard insert using the sound of the rolling marble to guide her. If it is too difficult, draw the different angles on a piece of paper to help.

What happens? The sound of the rolling marble and the length of time it takes to hit something are pieces of information our brain collects to give us a mental picture of the inside of the box.

Taste Test

This experiment shows the interdependency of our senses.

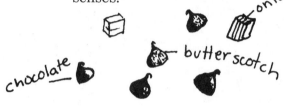

chocolate

onion

butterscotch

What you will need:

blindfold

baking chips in a variety of flavors: chocolate, peanut butter, butterscotch

tiny pieces of sweet onion

tiny pieces of apple

peanut butter

onion

apple

Blindfold the taste tester and have him plug his nose tightly. Place a tiny piece of apple or onion in his mouth and ask him to guess what it is. Test the different kinds of chips in the same way.

What happens? It is difficult to tell the difference between the chips and between the apple and the onion. The tongue is able to identify only salty, sour, bitter, and sweet. To really taste something, we need our sense of smell.

Touch Test

This experiment will surprise you! Even the most sensitive individual will have a hard time distinguishing the pressure of one pencil point from three on their forearm!

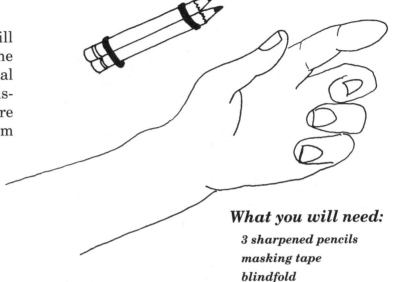

What you will need:

3 sharpened pencils
masking tape
blindfold

Tape two of the pencils together, making sure that the points are lined up evenly. Blindfold the person to be tested, and have her lay her arm palm up on a table. Gently touch her forearm near the elbow with a single pencil, two pencils taped together, or all three pencils at once. Ask how many pencils she feels. Change the number of pencils touched to the arm as you work your way down to the palm and fingers.

What happens? As the pencils move toward the palm, the number of nerve endings increases and a blindfolded person will be able to distinguish the number of pencil points, particularly on the tips of the fingers. Your forearm has fewer nerve endings, so it is more difficult to accurately gauge the number of pencil points there.

The Great Gong

This project dramatically demonstrates how our ability to hear relies upon detecting vibrations.

What you will need:

fishing line or kite string
metal spoon

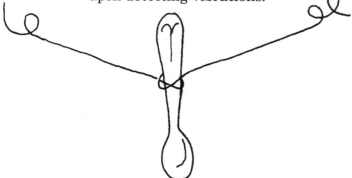

Take a length of fishing line and tie it to the spoon, leaving long enough ends to wrap around your fingers. Wrap your index fingers around each length of string and plug your ears with the string-wrapped fingers. Lean slightly over and gong the spoon against something hard, like a table.

What happens? The vibrations of the spoon hitting the table travel up the string and into your ears. The gong sounds loud, like a church bell. These vibrations hit the eardrum, where they continue to vibrate through bones and fluid, arriving finally at a nerve where your brain picks them up and interprets them as sound.

Lung Capacity Test

A simple device for measuring the amount of air your lungs can hold.

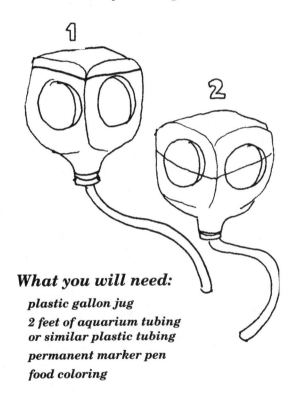

What you will need:

plastic gallon jug

2 feet of aquarium tubing or similar plastic tubing

permanent marker pen

food coloring

Fill the jug with water and add food coloring. This will make it easier to view the amount of air entering the container later. Fill a sink or dishpan halfway with water. Slip the tubing into the jug of water, then quickly and carefully turn the jug, tube and all, into the sink of water, upside down. Try not to let any air bubbles into the jug.

Take a regular breath and blow into the other end of the tubing. Make a mark on the jug where the water line is. Refill the jug with water and try it again, only this time take a deep breath and exhale fully into the jug.

What happens? When the exhaled air enters the jug, it pushes the water out, making it easy to measure lung capacity. Normally we use only about ⅛ of the capacity of our lungs. When we exercise or purposefully take a deeper breath, more air enters the lungs and is exhaled.

Fire Extinguisher

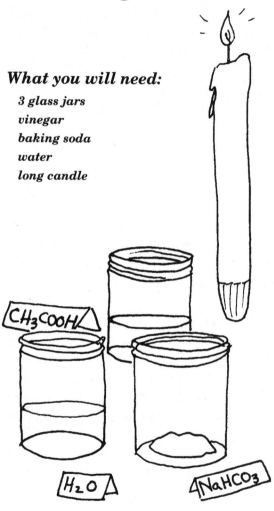

What you will need:

3 glass jars
vinegar
baking soda
water
long candle

The more dangerous, loud, messy, or unpredictable an experiment is, the more riveting to children. Although this is really none of the above when supervised, it is a sure hit!

Spread newspapers over your work area. Then have your child place a spoonful of baking soda into one jar, pour an inch or so of vinegar into the second jar, and fill the third jar half full with water. Light the candle and carefully hold it over the rim of each jar to see if each ingredient alone can extinguish the flame. Next, pour the vinegar into the water jar. Try again. Now add the soda to the water and vinegar mixture. Hold the flame over the rim of the jar without touching the liquid.

What happens? The flame is immediately extinguished by the invisible gas carbon dioxide. The slower and heavier carbon dioxide molecules shove the lighter oxygen molecules away from the flame and smother it. Without oxygen, it is impossible for a fire to burn.

Rising Water

We ended up doing this project many times over the course of a week, using different sizes of jars and numbers of candles. It is an endlessly interesting process to watch, and it piqued the curiosity of the whole family.

What you will need:

water
food coloring
candles
modeling clay
assorted jars
shallow glass casserole dish

Anchor the candle in the center of the dish with the modeling clay. Fill the glass dish two-thirds full with water and add a few drops of food coloring. Light the candle and slowly lower a jar over it. Leave the jar over the candle and watch!

What happens? Carbon dioxide is formed when oxygen in the air of the jar combines with carbon from the burning wax of the candle. Carbon dioxide is heavier and slower than oxygen and exerts less pressure on the water than the lighter and faster molecules from the outside air. This causes the water level to rise inside the jar higher than the water in the dish. Experiment with larger or smaller jars or try more than one candle. The more carbon dioxide produced, the higher the water will rise.

Science Shorts

No time in your family's busy schedule for science? These three projects take only a few minutes, but your kids will be delighted with the results.

Wintergreen Sparks

Many people know that cracking wintergreen Lifesavers in the dark gives off faint sparks, but do you know why?

Find a completely dark closet or room and place a wintergreen Lifesaver between your teeth or between the teeth of pliers. Crunch down with force while your child watches carefully for the bluish spark. Your child can also try it himself with a mirror held before his face as he bites.

What happens? There is energy stored in everything, and where the chemical composition allows it, it can be changed to light energy. Molecules in the wintergreen candy shift when pressure is applied, producing the quick glow you see. Cracking open certain types of rocks with a hammer will result in the same effect. (If your children want to try this, be sure to supply eye protection!) It is also interesting to note that some scientists believe many UFO sightings are actually light flashes from shifting rocks along continental fault lines.

Centrifugal Force in a Cup

I remember the magic of this one from my own childhood (using a half-filled pail of water), but I never knew the scientific principles that governed it. I do now, and so will you and your children!

What you will need:

paper cup for each child
string
water

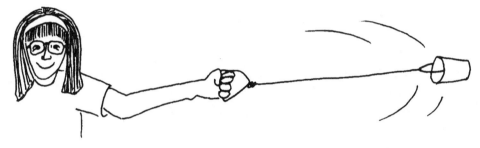

To make a string handle, poke a hole on opposite sides of the cup near the rim. Measure approximately 3 feet of string and thread it through both holes, then knot the ends at the top. Fill the cup halfway with water. Now for the fun part! Ask your children what will happen if you turn the cup upside down. (I bet the breakfast dishes on this one.) Then take the handle and spin the cup of water around in a big circle either above your head or at your side.

What happens? Centrifugal force keeps the water in the cup. By spinning the cup, you are applying a greater force on the water than the pull of gravity. Tides are caused on one side of the earth by the gravitational pull of the moon. The other side of the earth has a tidal bulge, stemming from the spin of the earth on its axis and on its journey around the sun. Gravity prevents the oceans from spinning off into space, while centrifugal force contributes to the pull of the tides.

115

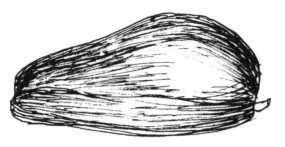

Air Streams and Apples

Children interested in airplanes and aerodynamics will love this project!

What you will need:
   apple
   popsicle stick or fork
   candle

Cut the apple in half from the stem down through the middle. Insert the popsicle stick or fork into one of the halves for a handle. Now light the candle. Have your child hold the apple beside the flame, a few inches away, with the flat side of the apple towards her. Ask her to blow on the flat of the apple and try and put out the candle flame. Turn the apple around so that the rounded side faces her. Now try and blow out the flame.

What happens? With the flat side toward you, the flame is difficult, if not impossible, to blow out. The flat side offers greater resistance to moving air. If you watch from the other side of the apple, you will see that the flame actually moves in toward the apple! When you blow against the rounded side, the shape is more streamlined and allows the air to move smoothly into the flame to extinguish it.

Smoke Prints

Yes, you can make a much faster, easier leaf print using ink or paint, but the process of this project is fascinating. We imagined that smoke prints provided the original drawing and writing tools for humankind.

What you will need:
glass soda bottle with a lid
candle
petroleum jelly
typing paper
newspaper
leaves

Fill the soda bottle with cold water and cap it. Spread a thin layer of petroleum jelly over one side of the bottle. To make the ink for your print, light the candle and hold the bottle with the petroleum jelly-side down over the flame. Roll the bottle back and forth, up and down over the flame so that a good layer of black carbon will collect over the jelly. When enough carbon has collected (this shouldn't take long), lay your leaf over it. Rub the leaf gently with your fingertips to collect enough carbon on its surface to print. Make sure the edges and center are covered.

Pull the leaf off the bottle, and place it carbon side up on the newspaper. Finally, lay a piece of typing paper over it and rub your fingers gently and completely over the leaf to transfer the carbon for a beautiful print.

117

M&M Science

This is science at its best—hands-on, interesting, and full of concepts that become deliciously clear.

R = Red
O = Orange
Y = Yellow
G = Green
B = Brown
T = Tan

What you will need:

1 package plain M&Ms per child

1 glass of water

white coffee filter

paper and colored marking pens

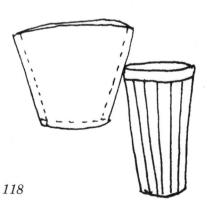

Your child should first feel the package of M&Ms before it is opened and make an estimate of how may candies are in the bag. Write down the estimate. Open the package and count the number of M&Ms. Write down the actual number. Now you are going to make a graph. Across the top of the paper write down the different colors of candies and draw lines down the paper separating each column. Find colored marking pens that match the colors of candies. With each candy counted in the color categories, make a mark with the pen. Don't eat them yet!

Strips of coffee filter

H₂O

When the graph is finished it is time to move on to the science of chromatography. Cut the coffee filter into two long sections. Next take two yellow, two green and two light brown M&Ms and place them on a small saucer. Take two red and two dark brown candies and place them on another saucer. Add 1 teaspoon of water to each saucer and stir the candies around in it until all the color is washed off. Now you can eat the wet ones! Take a strip of filter and place a third of its length onto the colored water of one saucer; repeat with the other strip of filter. Leave overnight or for several hours.

What happens? The dyes in the candies are absorbed by the filter at different rates, causing them to separate again on the filter (they will not separate into exactly the same colors of your M&Ms, however). This process is called "chromatography." Even though the colors were mixed together physically, the atoms and molecules actually remain separate in the water. Chromatography is the process that demonstrates this concept.

have m&m's for dessert. do the experiment. go to bed

next day look at the filter!

Outdoor Alternatives

Hula Hoop Bubble Ring

Hot day? Bored kids? This giant bubble ring creates an impressive wall of bubbles for an afternoon of fun!

To assemble your blower, lay the hula hoop on a flat surface. Fill the center with the embroidery hoops and plastic lid rings with their rims touching and as close to the edge of the hula hoop as possible. Don't worry if there are a few gaps and open spots in your hoop; it will still work.

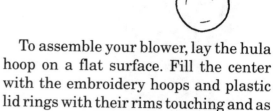

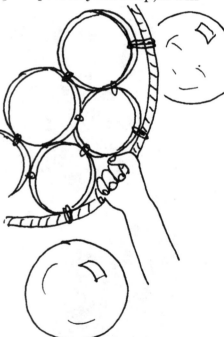

What you will need:

hula hoop

embroidery hoops or plastic lids with the center cut out, leaving a ring approximately 1 inch wide

cotton string

7 yards or so of cotton fringe

wading pool to dip the hoop into the bubble solution

bubble solution (see following recipe)

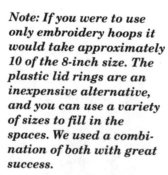

Note: If you were to use only embroidery hoops it would take approximately 10 of the 8-inch size. The plastic lid rings are an inexpensive alternative, and you can use a variety of sizes to fill in the spaces. We used a combination of both with great success.

Tie the lid rings and embroidery hoops together at their point of contact with short pieces of the cotton string. Next, secure the rings and hoops to the edges of the hula hoop. When you are finished, lift the hula hoop and check for rings that droop significantly more than the others. Retie if necessary.

For the final step, tie the cotton fringe over your hoop, looping it through the inner rings and the outer hoop. The fringe helps absorb and distribute the bubble solution and reduces the surface tension for an easier lift from the wading pool.

To use your Bubble Ring, pour the bubble solution into the wading pool. Dip the ring into the solution (dunking it on both sides the first time) and raise it into the breeze.

Bubble Solution

What you will need:

10 cups cold water

3 cups clear liquid dish soap (Dawn works best)

4 ounces glycerin (available at pharmacies)
You can also use 1 cup corn syryp, but glycerin makes longer lasting bubbles.

Pour the water into an empty 1-gallon container. Add the dish soap and glycerin and shake gently to mix. Allow to set for several hours, then pour into the wading pool.

Rainbow Chunky Chalk

Don't limit yourself to hopscotch. My kids have drawn highways, railroad tracks, small cities, and complicated games on our front walk. Making the chalk only adds to the fun! My thanks to Mary Welt for the recipe for this beautiful chalk.

What you will need:

4 paper tubes (The best size is from wrapping paper. It is narrower than toilet paper tubes.)

For each colored layer of chalk:

⅔ cup plus 2 tablespoons water

2 tablespoons tempera paint

⅔ cup dry plaster of paris

1 squirt of liquid dish soap

old plastic dish for mixing plaster

If you are using a wrapping paper tube, cut four 6-inch tubes from it. Tape one end of the paper tube closed with masking tape. Now you're ready to make the chalk. Mix the water, paint, plaster, and dish soap together in the plastic dish. Stir gently until mixed. The plaster should have the consistency of thick pancake batter. If it doesn't, add water to thin or a little more plaster to thicken the mixture. Fill the tubes one-third full with the plaster. Mix up another color, and pour this on top of the first layer. Add a third color, if desired. When the plaster has set, usually after several hours, peel off the tube. We have also poured the plaster into lightly greased candle molds with great success (bunny chalk!). Look around for other items that could yield interesting results.

The Magic Domain of a Fort

In most childhood recollections, there is a fort, a secret spot, or some claimed territory off-limits to adults. It is often the simple things that provide the best memories. A huge box, some pieces of lumber nailed together, or a bedsheet over a picnic table can offer your child more magic than any high-tech toy available on the market.

Almost all lumberyards and some hardware stores have bins of wood scraps they give away free. After perusing the bins, buy a sack of nails, add a hammer, and your child has all he needs for serious fort building. Or go to an appliance store for a refrigerator box. (Grocery stores also have watermelon boxes with lids that work beautifully.) Help your child cut out a door and some windows, if desired, and provide a can of spray paint or a can of paint and some brushes. If the fort painting is done outdoors in an appropriate place, this alone is a wonderful activity.

Grass Sleds

When that refrigerator box has broken down, use it to make a grass sled for sliding down grassy hills. Cut a piece of cardboard from the box big enough to sit on and long enough to fold over the feet and hang on to (picture a toboggan shape). Give your child a bar of soap to soap the bottom of the cardboard sled. Often the cardboard will slide without the soaping, but soaping makes the slickest sled around.

Once the cardboard is ready, find a grassy hill and slide away your troubles!

Plaster Cast Animal Tracks

Preserving a wild animal's tracks or even your own child's tracks with plaster of paris is great fun and incredibly easy! The trick is finding the tracks, but with sharp eyes, you and your family can discover a world at your feet, even in your own backyard. Birds, dogs, people, and cats often leave fine tracks to preserve, or make your own in a shoe box.

What you will need:

plaster of paris (available at hardware stores)
plastic bucket
water

126

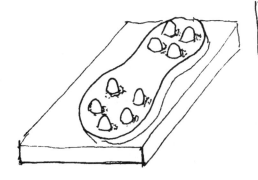

TRACK OF BIPEDAL HOMINID SPECIES
GLOBULUS CLEATUS
(BASEBALL CLEAT)

Find a track and clean out any loose debris by blowing lightly into it. If you are making your own tracks, line a shoe box with plastic, then mix together dirt and enough water to make a firm paste. Tracks dried in mud make the best forms to plaster cast (and mud is so fun to mix), but you can also get a fine print with compacted wet sand. Press the foot of your pet or child firmly into the damp mixture of mud or sand.

The next step is mixing the plaster in the bucket. If you want to mix the plaster precisely, follow the instructions on the box. We simply mix it to the consistency of pancake batter. Pour the prepared plaster into the track, allowing it to fill and spill over the track's edges. Wait for it to harden—it may take anywhere from five minutes to overnight, depending on the temperature and humidity—then gently dig beneath the plaster and lift the track. When the plaster has set 24 hours, use an old toothbrush to carefully brush away any loose soil or sand that may cling to the track.

Plaster casting animal tracks also makes a good science project. Look closely: What kind of creature made the track? How heavy would you guess its maker to be? What size? Old or young? Identify the tracks, mount them individually on shoe box lids, label them, and you have an excellent science fair project.

Snow Lanterns

If your climate has snow, create magic on a dark winter evening! Snow lanterns cast a wonderful luminous glow and are as much fun to make as they are beautiful to behold. Line your walk or driveway during the holiday season for a special welcome into your home.

What you will need:

snowballs

votive candle for each lantern

Help your child make large, firm snowballs and stack them in pyramid fashion around the votive candle. If you leave an open space at the top instead of making a "cave," the lantern will last longer. Our family uses the same form in a larger dimension to create snow forts and igloos.

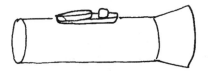

Night Walk

Shake up that old unwavering routine and take a night walk. Pick an evening with a full moon, and if you're feeling whimsical, surprise everyone and pull them out of bed. Supply individual flashlights, and even the littlest should feel safe (as long as there is a big hand to hold on to in the darkest parts!).

If you are lucky enough to have sidewalks, you can walk around your neighborhood, or drive to a school, tour the playground, and try out the monkey bars. If it is safe in your area, walk on the beach or in the park, or even around the high-school track a few times. If your area is unsafe after dark, drive to a lookout point and observe the moon together, or keep night walks in mind for the next vacation or camping trip.

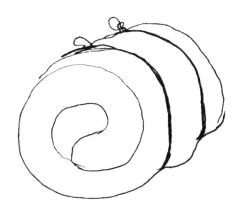

Backyard Camp Out

Get out those sleeping bags! Don't wait for the big camping trip! Join your kids on a hot night in the backyard and sleep under the stars. Check out a book on constellations from the library and pick out Orion, the Big Dipper, Polaris, and Cassiopeia. Pack up a midnight snack basket with popcorn, sliced apples, fruit juice, and maybe some fat chocolate chip cookies. Have the best vacation ever, in your own backyard!

Beach Candles

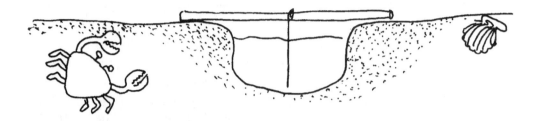

What you will need:

one block of paraffin per candle (available in the canning section of grocery stores)

crayons to color the wax

cotton string or wick

stick or pencil for each candle

sand: at the beach, at the river, or bought at a local nursery and poured into a large shoe box

large coffee can

small coffee can

If you have access to a beach, it is a perfect place for making candles. You don't have to worry about wax drips in your home, and there's a role for everyone, from making the beach fire to digging the forms in the sand. This activity was a memorable one for us. We not only made candles in the sand, but also poured the paraffin into seashells and the wondrous bulb of a seaweed called "kelp". Use your imagination! If there are no nearby beaches for this project, you can use sand in a large shoe box or the sand in a sandbox.

While you are waiting for the wax to melt, dig a hole in the sand the size of your desired candle. Hunt for treasures to fill—seashells, emptied crab shells, even washed up tin cans can make interesting candles. Make the wick by tying the cotton string to the middle of a stick. The length of the string should be the depth of your candle plus a couple of inches. You may want to tie a small weight to the opposite end of the string in order to make the wick lie straight in the wax.

When the wax is melted, add the crayon color of your choice for coloring your candle and let that melt, as well. Next, lay the stick or pencil across the top of your form, weighted side down, so the wick is held in place in the middle of the candle. Pour the melted paraffin into the form around the wick. Now for the hard part: Wait for the wax to cool and harden. When cool, cut wick from the stick and gently dig around the candle to lift your work of art from the sand. You may need to scrape the bottom of the candle with a pocketknife to level it.

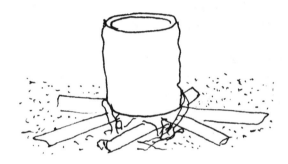

We made a beach fire to melt the wax for these candles. You could also use a stove. (Young children should be supervised!) While someone is getting the fire going, make a double boiler from the coffee cans by filling the large can one-third full with water and placing the smaller coffee can inside of it. Put the block of paraffin inside the smaller can and place your double boiler on the fire or stove.

Summertime Job Ideas for Kids

Summer is a perfect time for children to learn how to make money. Learning how to make money is an empowering process at any age, but particularly for older children who long for those expensive tennis shoes or a mountain bike that may be out of the reach of household budgets. My husband and I have always maintained that if our children were able to come up with half the money for their heart's desire, we would be willing to match it with the other half. But this means work above and beyond ordinary household chores. It means that the children have to be creatively ambitious and devise their own moneymaking projects. I am a hard but fair taskmaster. If the kids' lemonade stand is a resounding success, I make them pay a portion of their earnings for the materials they used.

Following is a list of a few of our kids' more successful summertime jobs, but keep an open mind! Your children may have unusual ideas of their own.

Outdoor Camps for Toddlers

This is an inspiring project, especially for children ten years and up. Have your child and a friend of hers organize a camp for one week (give it a special name, like "Camp Hands-On"), where parents can drop their toddlers off for two hours in the morning. Be sure to allow your child to create her own program that includes activities such as Play-Doh and simple crafts (your local library should have dozens of craft books to look over). The camp could also include songs, snacks, story time, or sandbox time. Water play and bubbles are also great fun for toddlers. Advertise to friends with toddlers and set a flat fee for the camp.

Gardening Services

Gardening provides a never-ending source of profit around our home. There is always planting, weeding, or watering to do, and I can always use help. Your child can distribute photocopied flyers around the neighborhood, offering services as a gardener, a lawn mower, or a sweeper for porches, decks, and sidewalks.

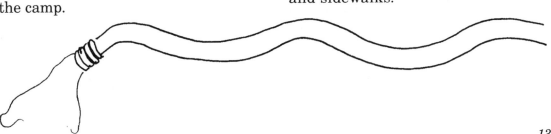

Lemonade Stands

Always a successful summertime venture! Include cookies or coffee, if desired. Make a big, colorful sign and set up the stand where foot or bike traffic is good.

Pet Services

When neighbors depart for vacations, who will take care of their pets? Your child can offer to feed and walk them. Photocopy a flyer advertising the services and distribute it in person around the neighborhood.

Vacation Services

Create a flyer to advertise the services your child can do for neighbors while they are on vacation. This could include not only care for pets, but watering the lawn, taking in the mail and newspapers, and turning on lights in or around the house.

Creativity for Sale

Sell flowers or vegetables from your garden at the local farmers' market. Create bubble blowers, make wind chimes from found objects, or bake brownies. Paint pictures on small canvases, make up craft kits with materials and instructions in Ziploc bags (check out books from the library for help). Don't be afraid to ask local art and craft shops if they would be interested in selling your wares.

Index